Chicago Secrets

J. Thomas Ganzer

ISBN 978-1-61225-232-2

Published by Mirror Publishing
Milwaukee, WI 53214
www.pagesofwonder.com

Printed in the USA

This book is dedicated to Angela. I never could have done this without your support and inspiration. Thanks for putting up with me during this mess.

Acknowledgements

Special thanks to all of my sounding boards, Emily, Jack, Mickie, Christine, Theresa, Becky, Nicole, and Sarah. Your creative input, edits, and even arguments, helped bring the characters to life. I am indebted to each and every one of you.

Cover model: Angela Navarrete Opazo
Cover photo (model): Front Room Photography
Cover photo (skyline): Monika Thorpe
Cover design: Group One Marketing, Menomonee Falls, WI

Chapter 1

Joe Haise sorted through the closet, silently stressing over his limited wardrobe. It was not exactly a Skittles rainbow of colors and textiles. Most federal prosecutors in the US Attorney's office in Chicago wore something eye-catching the day of closing argument; Joe was far too conservative to take part in that office tradition. He rubbed the sleep out of his eyes and struggled to focus on the task at hand. Joe, like most trial attorneys, didn't sleep for a week before *voir dire*, the process where attorneys question potential jurors in an effort to weed out the biased ones. Well, biased against them, anyway. But once the trial got under way, the evidence was admitted and the testimony was heard with little fanfare. The several million contingencies that Joe mentally prepared for never actually materialized (as they seldom do) and the case fell into a predictable rhythm. Gradually, his stress levels dropped as the witnesses said virtually what they were expected to say; the tense and shocking Perry Mason moments only happen on Perry Mason, and the Raymond Burr series went the way of the Dodo in 1966. Yesterday, Joe completed the submission of all the evidence, the defense attorney made a motion for a directed verdict of "not guilty" and, naturally, feigned shock when it was denied. Later this morning, after a brief but spirited defense, the attorneys will present their closing arguments, the judge will instruct the jury on the burden of proof and the jury will, at last, retire to deliberate.

Joe's jury had a particularly silly case to consider. An 88-year-old Bridgeport man named Earl McDonough was accused of fraud for allegedly exerting undue influence on Agatha, his 91-year-old new bride. Earl and Agatha lived in the same nursing home and met in the day room during Antiques Roadshow reruns. Agatha casually mentioned that she would never take her late husband's Waterford crystal collection to those crooks on television. Although Agatha managed to successfully avoid Earl's attention before, Earl was instantly smitten. Earl courted Agatha for a year while her body and mind slowly deteriorated. When she could no longer sign the rather large monthly checks from her late husband's pension, Earl decided it was time to pop the question. Because his heart was bursting with love (or atherosclerosis, or both), Earl declared their nuptials shall not wait another day. He called his 84-year-old pastor to the nursing home to wed them in front of two orderlies. The bride wore a white bathrobe and the couple served tapioca pudding and Clonazepam. Earl presented Agatha with his late wife's wedding ring (his first late wife, not his second) and a durable power of attorney. Tragically, on his way to take Agatha to the bank the following week, Earl ran a red light and was t-boned by an Oldsmobile on the passenger side, killing Agatha. Fortunately for Earl, she took out a $100,000 life insurance policy the day before the accident, naming Earl as the sole beneficiary. Earl might have eluded suspicion of any financial shenanigans, but in his capacity as the estate's personal representative, he had the temerity to file a $200,000 claim on behalf of Agatha's estate against his own auto insurer for his own negligent driving, essentially suing himself and, as the sole heir to Agatha's estate, collecting the proceeds. Joe couldn't prove Earl intentionally killed Agatha, but her signature miraculously appearing on the life insurance application when she couldn't write, and then depositing the application in the US Mail, was enough to charge Earl with federal mail fraud.

Joe selected a port-wine colored bow tie, he thought it was just enough color to impress the four women on the jury. Two of them were unemployed and one was a bookkeeper for her husband's business and was probably looking for something else to do for a week. The fourth was in pharmaceutical sales and was quite attractive – as pharmaceutical saleswomen tended to be. The eight men were all blue collar workers of one kind or another, no college degrees and a couple of tech school grads, but that was it. In this day and age, most people don't have the time for jury duty and look for any excuse to avoid it. Especially when it only pays $40 per day. Joe considered himself lucky if he landed one college degree in the jury pool. But old Earl made the case simple enough for even this

6

pool to grasp, so he felt pretty good about his chances. Joe figured Earl was probably hoping to die before the case actually went to trial but Joe was able to short-circuit some of the discovery and motion practice and, to everyone's surprise, Earl somehow managed to remain among the living (although Joe was certain he saw the Grim Reaper sitting in the back of the courtroom, staring at Earl and tapping his watch).

Having selected the appropriate tie, Joe picked an ivory white oxford shirt and dark gray suit. He owned one pair of cufflinks but never wore them to court. Juries seemed to resent an attorney who dressed better than they ever could. Joe was not exactly an imposing figure, he was just under six feet tall and weighed a modest 170 lbs. Well, maybe closer to 175. He had light brown hair and at 38 years old was beginning to lose some of it. He relied on his blue wire-rimmed glasses, the flashiest article he owned, being enough to distract the casual acquaintance from his gradually expanding waistline. He gave a quick polish to his black shoes and ventured downstairs. He entered the kitchen and saw his wife standing next to the sink. Tina had just made a pot of coffee and set out a muffin and smiled at Joe, as she always did in the morning when he came downstairs.

Tina was Joe's "little angel," and not just because of her diminutive stature. She stood barely over five feet tall and strived to maintain the figure of a dancer, a wonderful remnant of her days as a ballerina in college that earned her the moniker "Tina the Ballerina." She was also Joe's perfect match: demure, attentive and compliant. She founded a non-profit organization that helped low-income girls ages 8 through13 attend summer camp in the Wisconsin Dells, about four hours northwest of Chicago, called Her Way. Inner city girls whose family fit every stereotype – poor, absent father, unemployed mother, older brother in prison – spent a month in the summer camping, riding horses and generally escaping their circumstances for a brief time. The rest of the year Tina attended fundraisers around the Chicago area trying to finance the summer camp. In a good year, over 100 girls and a dozen volunteers could attend and for the last two years she has been able to hire a part-time intern and pay herself a not insignificant salary from the camp's coffers. Joe was still the primary breadwinner in the family of course, but Tina's salary was beginning to ease the pressure of paying a mortgage on a government lawyer's salary. Joe always surmised that Tina's inability to conceive a child of her own is what drove her to devote so much of herself to the summer camp.

This morning Tina wore her blonde hair up. She usually wore it in a bun but on those occasions when she needed to impress some donors she brushed her hair out, her hemline inched up and black pumps replaced the ballerina flats. Joe still admired how she maintained herself and he enjoyed picking her clothes out for her each morning while she complimented him on his taste. She was as pretty as the day they met and Joe thought they were a smart match. Their lives consisted of stereotypical suburban routine: work from 8-5, the first one home starts dinner and pours a single glass of wine for each, selected to compliment the entrée. After dinner, they both work on their laptops during the week and watch on-demand movies on the weekends. Sex was usually reserved for Saturday nights, although if Joe was in a frisky mood during the week dinner would occasionally get cold. During their newlywed phase, Tina would awkwardly propose something a bit kinky in bed, but Joe would blush and mutter something like, "Can you just imagine?" as they returned to their standard playbook. Still, he was as happy as anyone he knew and he did not regret his life for a moment.

"Oh my, you look handsome. Verdict today?" she asked.

"I have closing argument this morning, so we may have something by this afternoon."

"Is this the one with the old hustler?" Tina often lost track of Joe's cases and could only distinguish them by giving the defendants creative monikers.

"That's him. Case went in just fine, no surprises. Jurors didn't fall asleep, so I guess that means they actually paid attention."

"Well, good luck hon. Knock 'em dead." She gave Joe a kiss, grabbed her laptop and headed for the door. Joe grabbed a muffin and his travel mug and followed her out the door into the mild June sunrise. They climbed into their sensible cars, hers a silver VW Jetta, his a Toyota Corolla, and headed off in different directions. Joe had a long drive from Libertyville, a far northern suburb to the US attorney's Office for the Northern District of Illinois, located in downtown Chicago. It was a 45-minute drive on a good day, an hour most others, but for Chicago it was par for

8

the course. Tina worked at a small office in Waukegan which was a brief 15-minute drive northwest, and Joe was happy to make the sacrifice of a longer commute each day to accommodate her.

Joe fought the early morning traffic and arrived at his office just before 7:30 a.m. The courthouse was in the same building as the US Attorney's office, the Everett McKinley Dirksen United States Courthouse on Dearborn Street. US Attorney David Dunham, also known around the office as The Boss, ran a tight ship and expected all staff to be at their desks by 8:00am. Joe began reviewing his notes from the trial's first three days to prep his closing argument. He recalled various pieces of trial advice he received from his mentor, Lou Jackson, who guided him from an idealistic law school graduate to the mellow, thoughtful prosecutor he became. Lou was a larger-than-life figure, he weighed in at more than three full spins on the scale and liked to dress like a mob lawyer. Lou's wife came from money so he adorned himself with expensive watches and rings and believed he was a far better trial lawyer than he actually was. In reality, Lou worked about four hours a day and was virtually useless after a liquid lunch at the Exchequer Pub, a bar a few blocks from the courthouse. Joe accompanied Lou on these midday excursions when he first joined the prosecutor's office and Lou would regale Joe with war stories and pearls of wisdom. He liked to tell Joe that the Exchequer referred to an English court of equity in the 19th century, which is why he spent so much time there. But after the third or fourth time Lou imparted this same bit of trivia, Joe realized that Lou was an alcoholic burnout who simply liked to spend his waning years in the law drinking top shelf bourbon and holding court with young lawyers. But Lou paid his dues over the course of his career and his advice was well-taken.

After an hour, Joe packed up his briefcase and walked out of his office. The staff had filed in while he prepped his closing, so there was a buzz in the office. Any time one of the prosecutors had a trial, it was not unusual for the other prosecutors and staff to meander down a few floors to the courtroom to watch closing arguments. Joe's secretary was Ellen Dawes; she was 50 and was something of a clichéd government worker - smart enough, but not a genius. Her desk was in the main reception area, consequently everyone walked past her desk as they came and went. Ellen worked exactly 40 hours per week, she arrived at 8:00am, took a standard lunch, and left at precisely 5:00 p.m. Joe shared Ellen with four other prosecutors, but he liked to do most of the work himself so she did not do much for Joe other than some letter writing.

"I saw you had your door closed and I didn't want to bother you. Is the closing argument this morning?" Ellen asked.

"Yep, evidence came in pretty much as expected," Joe replied.

"Well, that's good news. I have the letters ready to go in the tax fraud case in case you want to sign them now."

Joe was miffed. He had his briefcase in one hand, a notepad in the other, and was heading to a closing argument in a federal fraud trial. Ellen, being Ellen, could only comprehend that some letters needed to be signed and could see no farther than her own nose.

"Well, Ellen, let me just finish this trial first and I can sign them right after," he replied somewhat tersely.

"Oh, ok. I guess that will be fine," she replied, as if she had some say in the matter. Joe tolerated her because her spelling and punctuation were flawless, but since the advent of the word processor and the spell check, her utility to the office had decreased exponentially. But she was like all federal employees - completely and totally unfireable. Joe was stuck with her until she retired in precisely 10 years. Ellen often announced, unprompted, that she would retire at age 60 and not a day later (or a day sooner, unfortunately for Joe).

Joe arrived in the courtroom, quietly passed through the small wooden gate separating the gallery from the attorneys, and settled in at counsel table. Old Earl was already there with his attorney and looked up as Joe walked in. Earl was used to charming his way out of trouble, and like all gregarious defendants, he probably assumed that being pleasant to Joe would magically make the charges disappear. Earl, despite his years, was pretty sharp. He dressed like a poor old widower at trial, sporting shabby brown pants held up by a pair of black suspenders, a beige golf shirt buttoned all the way up, and a sweater that was usually buttoned improperly. He played up the role in front of the jury, hobbling around when the jury was present and feigning confusion when his attorney would show him copies of the exhibits. He also nodded off once or twice during the trial, but Joe wasn't too sure he was faking that. Earl decided not to testify. Even the most confident and charming defendants refused, knowing they were never smarter than the prosecutor questioning them.

Earl stood up and bellowed across the courtroom. "Well, there you are Mr. Joe! Not movin' fast, not movin' slow!"

"Hello Mr. McDonough, good to see you again," Joe responded with a slight smile. Earl's attorney stood behind Earl and rolled his eyes as his client went into full Earl-mode. Joe stifled a laugh and reached over to shake the attorney's hand.

"Hello Mr. Scott," Joe said gravely. Joe had several trials with Rich Scott over the years and found him to be a tough advocate, but eminently reasonable in every respect.

"Mr. Haise," he responded curtly. Years ago Lou explained to Joe that you can never be informal or pleasant when greeting an attorney in front of their clients. Most defendants have little faith in the justice system to begin with, and watching their attorney glad-hand their taxpayer-funded executioner will only serve to foster the paranoid belief that the fix was in. So the attorneys all engage in various displays of contempt and derision when they confront each other in the courthouse and the back-slapping simply waits until they trade drinks at the bar after the case is concluded. A number of people filed in to the courtroom and seated themselves in the gallery. No one appeared the entire trial in support of Earl, which depressed Joe a bit. Maybe he truly loved Agatha, or maybe he truly loved her money. Either way, he lost three wives and had no emotional support during what was the most trying time he has ever endured in his 88 years. The only attendees were a handful of folks from Joe's office and a few law students completing some course requirement. Ellen never came, since watching a trial is not explicitly stated in her job description. The judge peered out from his chambers at the assembled crowd and nodded to the clerk. The clerk stood and recited the standard speech, "All rise. This court is now back in session. The Honorable Marion Henry Matthews presiding."

Chapter 2

Marion Matthews is an exceptional Federal District judge. He has been on the bench since Joe joined the US Attorney's office over a decade ago and has a supreme grasp of the law. At 62 years old, he has flowing white hair and at least another 10 years left in him. Every attorney knows Judge Matthews doesn't suffer fools gladly, any attorney who tries to make a spectacle out of his courtroom finds themselves quickly embarrassed and the message is sent. One of Joe's first trials, shortly after arriving in the US Attorney's office in 2001, involved a federal highway official named Giuseppe Decarlo who steered toll road improvement projects to his cousin-in-law in exchange for a modest "referral fee." Giuseppe spent the money on the necessities of life: a new Cadillac SUV, several trips to Italy, and breast implants for his wife.

Joe was a greenhorn right out of law school and had no idea what to expect. During that trial, Giuseppe's lawyer Mario Rossi thought it would be a great idea to explain to the jury that his client simply did what Illinois politicians do every day. He asked the judge - in the presence of the jury, naturally - to issue a subpoena to Jim Edgar, Governor of Illinois, to explain how government employees rewarding friends and family members with lucrative contracts was an accepted practice in Illinois. Judge Matthews, to Joe's recollection, appeared to briefly consider throwing a gavel at Rossi's head. Instead, he asked the attorney, "Counselor, are you telling me your client broke the law and cost the taxpayers of Illinois millions of dollars, but he should be excused because *everyone else* does it? If the Governor jumped off a bridge, would your client do that too? If he wants to reconsider his plea, we can certainly do that. Should I excuse the jury?"

Mario was befuddled trying to process what he was supposed to do next. The jury heard the judge ask if Mario wanted to change his client's plea to the most indefensible position in the history of jurisprudence: *Reus Cum Explicatione*, or "Guilty – With an Explanation." Mario muttered something about needing a minute to confer with his client. The judge gave the parties a 10-minute recess, and Mario nearly dropped to his knees in the hallway and begged Joe for a deal. Joe took pity and agreed to recommend 18 months in Pekin Federal Correctional Institution, south of Peoria. Mario, practically in tears, thanked him and dutifully reported to Giuseppe that the judge has it in for him and the sonofabitch prosecutor wanted three years in a maximum security prison. But, Mario explained, because he threatened to subpoena the Governor, the prosecutor backed down and agreed to recommend 18 months in order to avoid the scandal from the Governor having to explain the concept of "graft" to the jury. Giuseppe hugged Mario and declared him the greatest lawyer ever before walking into the courtroom and pleading guilty.

Joe shook off the memory of the Decarlo trial and returned to Earl. After some preliminary maneuvering by the attorneys, Judge Matthews brought in the jury and gave them lengthy instructions for the deliberations, which explained the concept of fraud, intent and reasonable doubt. The judge then nodded to Joe to begin his closing argument. Joe grabbed a few pages of notes he had no intention of referring to and placed them on the podium in front of the jurors. Lou Jackson once told Joe that one should never plan the closing argument in advance, as you don't know how the evidence will come in. But once the trial is over, the closing argument writes itself with every thought you developed throughout the trial. Lou was right of course. The closing argument is simply reminding the jury of the high points of your case. It takes little preparation, a bit of flair, and above all, it should be brief. The jury heard the same testimony the attorneys did and the jurors were usually anxious to begin deliberations, spending three hours reminding them of what they all heard serves no useful purpose. The jury tunes out the attorneys after ten minutes anyway, so Joe would simply hit the high notes and walk off, stage right.

Joe began by thanking the jurors for their patience and explained that he took no pleasure in prosecuting someone of Earl's advanced years. However, he said, mail fraud was a serious offense and Mr. McDonough

13

should not be excused simply because he chose to commit the offense so late in life. He walked them through the testimony. Agatha's physician and nurses testified about her inability to communicate, much less read and sign a legal document. The FBI agent testified about the insurance policy payout, and the forensic expert testified about the signature being different from anything Agatha ever signed before. Joe had to use a soft touch, Earl was a sympathetic defendant and Joe would win no points by crucifying him to this jury. The women likely empathized with Earl, and the men typically hated the heavy hand of the federal government even more than they hated criminals. Joe summed up by allowing the jury to feel bad for Earl, but convict him nonetheless. After spending a few minutes going over the key pieces of evidence, Joe steeled himself for his closing speech. "Folks," Joe loved calling the jury 'folks,' "I don't relish being here, any more than anyone else wants to be here. But I have a job to do, and that job is to prosecute people like Mr. McDonough who break the law. And you have a job to do, evaluate the evidence and render a verdict based on that evidence. We don't have to decide if Mr. McDonough is a good person or not, we only have to decide whether Mr. McDonough signed Agatha's name on that insurance application. We can all come to the conclusion that Mr. Mc-Donough, beyond a reasonable doubt, committed the offense of fraud, as charged in the indictment. Thank you."

Joe was certain to make eye contact with each juror as he recited the final few sentences, and even threw in a knowing wink as he thanked them. Not seeing any heavy eyelids, he was content he did as well as could be expected and returned to counsel table. Rich Scott rose and began his closing. He made a few good points, no one actually *saw* Earl - he used his client's first name throughout, a good tactic to humanize his client to the jury- sign the application. The doctor and nurses admitted Agatha had good days and bad and that her ability to write was declining, so of course the signature would look different on the insurance application. Rich was animated and made grand gestures as he spoke and he seemed to have the jury's rapt attention. He locked his gaze on the jury and pounded the podium as he spoke, making an impassioned plea for justice. His voice rose to a crescendo as he steered the jury's eyes to Earl and asked rhetorically: "Weren't the actions of the heavy-handed federal government in forcing

14

an elderly, innocent man of meager means who just lost his beloved wife and now must sit through the humiliation of a trial, enough of a punishment?" Joe contemplated objecting to the last statement, but it is considered somewhat unprofessional to object during an opposing attorney's closing argument. There is a courthouse legend that Judge Matthews once ordered an attorney to perform 1,000 hours of *pro bono* work as punishment for unnecessarily objecting during a closing argument, thus, Joe sat silent. Joe hoped the jury would see through Rich's hollow theatrics and appreciate Joe's more cerebral presentation.

The judge charged the jury and the bailiff led them to the deliberation room just before lunch. The court went into recess and Earl and Rich Scott made for the hallway to let Earl get some rest. Joe went back up to the office. The clerk would call him and Rich Scott when the jury came in with a verdict or had a question. Joe tried to get some work done. He signed the letters Ellen prepared, much to her satisfaction. Ellen was incapable of displaying any emotion resembling "delight," so "satisfaction" was as good as it got. A few other Assistant US Attorneys stopped by Joe's office for the predictable post-mortem analysis, telling Joe he did a great job with a lousy case, that he should be proud of himself, he shouldn't worry about what the jury does, etc. Joe made the same exact speech to his colleagues when they were awaiting a verdict, so he accepted their words with grace.

Finding it difficult to concentrate, Joe surfed the internet and rearranged some files on his desk. He calculated the jury would first order their free lunch and then elect a foreman while they waited for the food. Then they would eat and start deliberations in earnest. They would reach a verdict around 4:15 p.m., but they would ask the bailiff for dinner menus first. After receiving dinner on Uncle Sam, they would announce a verdict sometime after 5:30 p.m. Joe was confident about the verdict. The jury had to see that Earl forged Agatha's name for his own financial gain. What other verdict could they reach? Joe decided to walk over to the Exchequer and grab a sandwich.

He strolled in and grabbed a seat at the bar. The bartender was a young guy, probably one of the million recent college graduates who couldn't find a job in Chicago and is bartending until something better

15

comes along. Joe ordered a turkey and avocado club and an ice water. He set his phone on the bar so he wouldn't miss the clerk's call and waited. Two twentysomething girls walked in and took seats at the bar around the corner, close enough that Joe was forced to listen to the excruciating banality of their conversation. They were young and cute and the bartender immediately began flirting with them. Joe was annoyed and resented having to be subject to the pathetic ritual. He recalled how he met Tina at a Legal Aid mixer seven years earlier. Joe was the US Attorney's designee at the function, sent to talk about the importance of quality representation for the indigent in the federal court system. Tina was there to try to raise some seed money for the girls' camp she was hoping to start the next year and was trying to woo some law firms looking for a charitable pet project. They hit it off immediately. Joe was uncertain why someone as lovely as Tina would be talking to him. Tina later confessed that Joe's attention to her every thought was something she had not experienced and she found it fit her quite nicely. She let Joe know that she would be interested in seeing him again if he asked. Joe nearly missed the hint but the light went on and Joe asked her out.

Joe finished his sandwich and settled up with the bartender. He walked out in the mild afternoon sun and began the trek back to the office. Joe wanted to win this trial, but he didn't really *need* it. He is on a solid career track at the US Attorney's office. He is scheduled to get a raise each of the next two years, and then he could move up to Financial Crimes Section Head when Lawrence "Suds" Milder retires - or his liver gives out, whichever comes first. He and Tina talked about adopting children last year, she is 34 and he is 38, but Tina seemed preoccupied with work and Joe didn't push the issue. He assumed she would warm up to the idea, but she hasn't brought it up recently. Their life was stable and predictable, and he was glad he could offer her that.

Back at the office Joe started looking at a new financial case. A community center that received millions in federal block grants had trouble explaining to its board of directors where $250,000 went. A forensic accountant was able to determine the Executive Director's secretary made checks out to herself, cashed them, booked them as payments to various insurance companies, then doctored the .pdf copies of the checks and placed them in the accounting file. It wasn't until a temp worker came in while the secretary was out on maternity leave that the fraud was discovered. A quick call to the insurance companies revealed that they had no policies with the company and the secretary was arrested three days after giving birth. Joe was so far into the file that he lost track of time when the phone rang at quarter to five.

"Mr. Haise, this is Judge Matthews's clerk. The jury just came back with a verdict."

"Thank you, I'll be right down." Joe packed up his briefcase and headed out the door. Ellen was already packing up for the evening, she wouldn't stay for the verdict. Joe was a little more intense now, the rest of the staff could sense his unease and gave him a wide berth. Joe arrived in the courtroom five minutes later and was the first one there. The clerk was shuffling papers and the judge was in chambers. Earl and Rich Scott had yet to arrive, so Joe settled in at counsel table and drummed his fingers on the arm of the chair. After a somewhat nerve-wracking ten minute wait, Earl and Rich Scott walked in. Earl was more ashen-faced than he had ever been and for the first time there was no grand greeting for Joe. After settling in, the clerk pushed a buzzer under her desk and the judge emerged shortly after. The clerk began to make the announcement, but all she got out was "All ri-", before the judge arrived and cut her off, waiving everyone back to their seats. Judge Matthews asked if there was any business to take up before the jury came in.

"Nothing from the prosecution your honor," Joe said.

"No, your honor. My client is a bit tired, so perhaps we can take up any additional business on another day." Rich was coyly referring to continuing Earl's bail until the sentencing, if Earl is found guilty. This was a pretty standard request, and it was clear Rich didn't want to agitate his client any more than he already was by spelling it out for him.

"No objection your honor," said Joe. Earl looked confused by the exchange, but Rich patted him on his arm and told him it was just some "legal mumbo-jumbo" and he didn't need to worry.

The jury was brought in and seated. If Earl was expecting a lot of preparation and fanfare, he would be disappointed. The judge merely asked if they reached a verdict, they all nodded and the foreperson - the attractive pharmaceutical rep - stood and handed the verdict form to the bailiff, who relayed it to the judge. Judge Matthews displayed his best poker face while reading it and stated that it appeared in order.

"Mr. McDonough, please stand," the judge said dutifully. Rich helped Earl to his feet and for the first time, Earl looked like he may just die right then and there.

"I will now read the verdict. 'We the jury, in the case of United States versus Earl McDonough hereby find as follows: The defendant is Not Guilty of the crime of mail fraud as charged in the indictment."

Earl seemed confused and Rich had to hug him and smile, telling him they won. Earl slumped down in his chair and sat stone-faced. Joe felt like he got punched in the gut, but had been through enough trials to know you never show emotion to the jury. Not because the jury members will care, Joe will never see them again. But the judge will, the clerk will, and Rich Scott will And your reputation is your stock in trade in legal circles.

The judge asked Joe if he wanted to poll the jury, he declined. The judge thanked the jury for their service and dismissed them. Everyone rose as the jury was escorted out, but Joe couldn't bear to look the jurors in their eyes.

The judge asked if there was anything else, Joe mumbled, "No your honor." Rich Scott said "no," and the judge declared court adjourned. Everyone began packing up, but Joe was still a bit shell shocked. He felt a hand on his shoulder, it was Rich Scott.

"Good job, Joe. I guess this makes us even for the Lopez trial." Joe got the best of Rich several years ago in a tax evasion case.

"Yep. Darn, I thought I had this one," Joe said.

"Well, I think I had it when Agent Stark conceded no one at the nursing home actually saw Earl sign her name to the insurance form. The jurors looked like they really wrapped their brains around that. No witness, no crime."

"I guess I assumed the jury would make the connection without an eyewitness," Joe said.

Earl managed to get up out of his chair and walk over to Joe. Joe steeled himself for some gloating, but Earl was surprisingly contrite. "I'm sorry you had to go through all this fuss, young man. I didn't know everyone would go through all this trouble just for me."

"Well, I'm glad we finally got through all of it and we can move on." Joe was in no mood to lecture Earl. Besides, Joe knew the insurance company would still dispute Earl's claim to the policy proceeds in civil court. They would simply wait him out for a few years until he dies and keep the money.

Joe shuffled out of the courtroom and loosened his bow tie in the elevator. He walked back to the office, closed his door and plopped in his chair. Most of Joe's colleagues cleared out at 5:00 p.m., but a few attorneys still lingered. No one stopped to ask him how it went, they probably knew the verdict about one minute after he left the courtroom. The clerks' network rivaled anything the NSA had in place.

Joe did a mental autopsy of the trial. Rich Scott offered no real surprises, but Joe realized he underestimated Earl and his "sweet old man" routine. The jury frustrated Joe, but he couldn't really blame them. They didn't know that most crimes have no eyewitness, instead, prosecutors cobble together the case from bits of evidence to create a picture. The fact that no one saw Earl forge Agatha's name shouldn't matter, the remainder of the evidence was overwhelming. But the jurors' frame of reference had become modern day television. CSI taught them that prosecutors have all sorts of blue glowing lights that conclusively prove who killed the stripper, which, unfortunately for Joe, never happens in actual trial practice.

Chapter 3

Joe waited until everyone cleared out and then left the office and headed to his car. He caught some late traffic and didn't get home until 7:00 p.m. Joe could smell the pizza baking in the oven as he walked in the door. Tina usually took the time to whip up something, but Joe deduced she must have had a long day to simply surrender to the pizza gods.

"Hon, I'm home," Joe called. He heard Tina yell something from the bedroom; he started to pour himself a glass of wine while waiting for her. Tina came down wearing sweats and a t-shirt.

"Long day, hope a pizza is okay. I didn't get to the store, had a late meeting with a potential donor." Tina seemed tired and a bit distracted. He could tell when she was a little out of it.

"That's fine, hon. I need to get changed and relax. Traffic was brutal."

"Hmm," Tina replied. "How was your day?" she asked absentmindedly.

"Well, jury came in a few hours ago," Joe responded plainly.

"Oh my god, the trial! I totally forgot, what happened?"

"Jury found him Not Guilty around 5:00." Joe was unhappy about the verdict and the fact that Tina forgot he had a trial was an additional frustration he didn't need at the moment.

"Well, they got it wrong, in my opinion. That old hustler got away with one." Tina spoke while she took the pizza out of the oven and rifled through drawers for the pizza cutter. Tina didn't seem too concerned with Joe's loss. She used to give him a big hug and take him out for a cocktail and some dessert when he lost a case. They would talk about the trial and she would express shock that the jury could acquit someone in the face of such overwhelming evidence, and Joe would feel some measure of reassurance in his trial skills. But tonight she seemed content to offer a few words of encouragement and a slice of pizza. Joe headed upstairs, quickly changed and came back down.

Joe asked Tina about her day and she talked in generalities about the summer camp and everything that needed to be done before it starts in six weeks. She used to go up to the camp for the month but would come back one or two days each week to recharge her batteries; she trusted the staff members and youth volunteers on site to handle the girls when she wasn't there. The past two years she stayed at the camp for the entire month as the number of campers increased to the point that it was considered one of the more reputable non-profits in northern Illinois. Joe would hold down the fort until Tina got through the month and finally arrived home, exhausted but exhilarated. She would take a long shower, sleep for a few days, and they would get back to some semblance of a normal life.

Tina grabbed a couple plates and set them on the cooking island. Their house was a modest two story, three bed, 2.5 bath Colonial. They house-hunted for six months armed with a small, but critical, list of must-haves, and resigned themselves to work on completing the rest of the improvements over the next 30 years. They bought a foreclosure property on the cheap and spent the leftover house budget making it as nice as they could manage. Joe got what he wanted in the kitchen: gray granite countertops, double wall oven, cooking island with a sink, white subway tile backsplash and stainless steel appliances. Tina got her wish list as well: king-size four poster bed with a white feather comforter, faux-Italian marble in the master bath, clawfoot bathtub, a standing shower with double showerheads on opposite walls, and his-and-hers above-counter bathroom sink bowls. Joe was amazed at what Tina could scavenge at second hand stores and estate sales. The basement was unfinished and the guestroom had a queen-size bed, second-hand dresser and nothing else. The third bedroom became Tina's sparse office; Joe did his work on his laptop in the living room while he listened to music.

Joe moved some barstools around the cooking island and poured more wine as they both settled in around the corner of the island. Tina loved to shop at a gourmet grocer in Mundelein. It cost quite a bit more

21

but you could actually taste the food. She confessed that she picked up an organic spinach-feta pizza two days earlier and buried it in the back of the fridge hoping it would escape Joe's attention until one evening when they were both too tired to cook. The pizza had a bold, tangy sauce with a healthy dose of oregano and a few cloves of garlic. Joe busied himself setting the places, wiping the flatware and straightening the napkins He prided himself on his old-world manners and Tina's impeccable etiquette made her a perfect complement for him. Joe finally declared the meal ready and they dove in. They talked little and ate quickly, Joe detested speaking during dinner. Joe spied a drop of sauce dangling precariously from the corner of Tina's perfect mouth. He paused and wiped the corners of his mouth pointedly, but Tina missed the hint and continued to eat. Slightly miffed, Joe cleared his throat and peered over his glasses while wiping his mouth again. Tina looked up from her plate, plucked her napkin from her lap and dabbed the corners of her mouth with a slight smile.

Tina only had two slices, she was always watching her figure. "I don't want to look like a fat ballerina," she would say. She had attended Bryn Mawr where she majored in Romance Languages. She wanted to concentrate on ballet, but was told repeatedly that she was too short to ever pursue a career as a performer, so she danced for fun and studied French and Italian. After graduation, she applied for a marketing position with a number of touring dance companies and a few international fashion houses, hoping to parlay her Italian and French background into something that required her to divide her time between Rome, Paris and Chicago. But the phone never rang and she came back down to earth, used her linguistic background to secure an internship and then a full-time job at an adult literacy center, and eventually formed her summer camp.

After dinner Joe did a full recap of the day's events, telling Tina how Old Earl nearly keeled over, but then apologized to Joe for causing so much commotion. Joe resigned himself to the verdict and was already starting to think about the next case, anything to get the taste of the loss out of his mouth. Tina listened, not too intently, asked a few questions and finally said she needed to get on the computer to line up some insurance policies for the camp next month. Joe would review the boilerplate language of the policies. He liked that he was able to guide her through

22

the complexities of insurance procurement. Tina retired to her office with a glass of wine and Joe grabbed a second glass for himself and put on a David Gray CD. He popped open the laptop and began working, first checking the Chicago Tribune website to see if his case made it in the paper. It did not. He emptied the last of the wine when he heard his phone chirp from the kitchen, signaling the arrival of a text message. Joe rarely gave out his phone number and his secretary Ellen never gave it out. Still, Joe got the occasional spam text or a message from a wrong number. He sighed and carefully placed his glass on the coffee table and the laptop on the floor, and lumbered to the kitchen.

He picked up the phone and checked the text. It read, "Alessandra, do you have any available appointments this week?" Joe furrowed his brow and put the phone back down. It was Tina's phone, which was identical to Joe's. He searched for his phone, realized he left it in the bedroom, and headed upstairs. He peeked in the office and saw Tina working at her computer, she didn't hear Joe with her headphones on and he quietly slipped out and grabbed his phone from the bedroom. Tina emerged from the office and Joe met her in the hall.

"You got a text hon, some wrong number." Joe gave her a quick kiss on the forehead.

Tina forced a bit of a laugh and said, "Yeah, I'm always getting those." She accompanied Joe downstairs and made a bee-line for her phone. She checked the text message and said, "Huh. Beats me." She tucked the phone into her waistband and headed back upstairs. Joe settled back on to the sofa, grabbed his laptop and put his feet up on the coffee table.

After a few hours, Joe was tired and lonely; he shut down the laptop and headed upstairs for the night. Tina emerged from the office and the two wordlessly prepared for bed. After the various bedtime rituals were completed, Tina emerged from the bathroom and slid in bed beside Joe. Two glasses of wine was enough to get Joe in the mood for romance, but after two years of dating and five-plus years of marriage, he still didn't quite know what excited her. She rolled over on her side, away from Joe, and he spooned with her to signal his interest. She rolled over and gave him a kiss and he slid her pajamas off. Within minutes they were naked, Joe was on top and they were in the moment. Tina panted quietly, and begged

23

Joe to climax. "Come on, hon. Come on, come on," over and over until Joe obliged. Tina did not always lose herself the way Joe did, but Joe read an article that said some women simply prefer to remain in control of themselves and that sex may not be that important to them. Joe hung his hat on this bit of trivia and convinced himself that he and Tina still had a far more fulfilling marriage than most couples.

Joe quickly fell asleep and drifted off into a dream. He was back at the trial and he saw Earl across the courtroom sneering at him. He kept muttering to Joe, "I won, you lost. You are a chump. You didn't see it coming, did you? Open your eyes. Wake up. Wake up!" He awoke with a start around 2:00am and looked around, Tina was not in bed. He stumbled around in the dark and found the door. The floor creaked as he walked down the hallway and he saw a light under the door coming from Tina's office. He opened the door and saw Tina looking at him, quite alert and bright eyed considering the late hour.

"Hi hon! Couldn't sleep?" she asked.

"No, had a weird dream. You still working at this hour?"

"Oh yeah. I had some insurance stuff to look at." Joe thought Tina was overly cheerful. She had the rest of the bottle of wine they started at dinner sitting next to the monitor and a near-empty glass. Joe knew she would work at the computer with a small glass of wine from time to time, but this was a bit odd. Perhaps the stress of the camp was getting to her and she was drinking a bit more than usual.

"Can you come back to bed?" Joe asked.

"Oh sure, I was just finishing. Go back to bed and I will power down." Joe turned to leave but noted that Tina continued to look at him, and not the monitor, until he finally left the office and went back to the bedroom. When he climbed into bed, he could hear the singsong of the computer shutting off before Tina walked in and climbed into bed. He made a mental note to take her out to dinner this weekend to help her decompress from all the stress of the summer camp preparation.

Chapter 4

Joe drummed his fingers on the steering wheel as he drove to work the next day. Traffic was unusually heavy and he turned on 670-The Score and listened to the hosts drone on about how much the Cubs were paying for mediocre pitching. Joe zoned out. He remembered back when he and Tina began courting. He took it slow for the first few dates. He did extensive research on the best places to take a first date in Chicago, the best places for a second date, and most importantly, the best places for a third date. Joe read the accompanying article and apparently the third date is when a young couple is supposed to consummate the relationship. Joe thought it was a little much for only a third date. After all, he was still getting to know Tina, so he picked several places from the second date list and used them for the subsequent dates.

Tina always greeted him in slacks and a blouse for their dates, he liked that she dressed conservatively. Joe had a few dates with women who dressed a bit loose, but they never interested him much and actually made him somewhat ill-at-ease. He was comfortable with Tina, and on the first few dates they talked for hours, Joe about his job and Tina about her experiences trying to break into a ballet company or the fashion and modeling industry as a personal assistant. She regaled him with stories about waiting in long lines for job interviews, how she once saw Cindy Crawford in the ladies room when she was taking a tour of a fashion house, and all the chic outfits the models wore. Joe wasn't much interested in the topic but Tina was so adorable that he listened intently. She absolutely shined when she talked and Joe memorized every inch of her face, arms, shoulders, everything. Tina noticed that Joe couldn't take his eyes off her and she seemed to revel in the attention Joe showered on her.

After five dates, a lot more kissing, and one awkward attempt by Tina to undo her blouse before Joe told her it was "too soon," they made love for the first time. Joe loved every minute of it and repeatedly told Tina how gorgeous she was. Tina constantly asked Joe if he enjoyed it, if he thought she was good, if she was pretty. They made love often in the first few months and Joe eventually proposed. It wasn't a terribly romantic proposal, he simply dropped to a knee and popped the question before they went out to dinner one night. She screamed and said yes. He couldn't ask her father for permission since he died when Tina was a toddler and she had no siblings. Her mother worked as a secretary for a small Catholic school and Sunday church was a ritual growing up, but Tina stopped going to mass when she was in college.

Tina wanted a bigger wedding than Joe could afford so they were forced to settle for a small, civil ceremony. Joe felt it worked out for the best because Tina only had a few guests at the wedding, just three college friends and her mother. Tina was just adorable in her wedding dress; it was white, of course, strapless with a small train. She told Joe how it was almost exactly like a Vera Wang dress she saw, but Joe confessed he didn't know who that was. She wore high heels to appear more statuesque and Joe thought she was a vision. Tina's eyes darted around the crowd, silently begging for admiration from the assembled guests as she started her walk down the aisle. The small gathering rose and watched her every movement and she appeared to bathe in the attention. Her mother cried during the ceremony, she must have been so proud. Joe thought Tina appeared a bit embarrassed by her mother's awkward display, almost ashamed even. But they all got through the ceremony and reception and had a wonderful honeymoon in Corpus Christie. Joe wanted to take her to Paris, but he was only a few years out of law school and was burdened with student loans.

The first few years of marriage were pure bliss, despite their many struggles. They lived in a small apartment and rarely went out. Though they were poor, they were truly happy. Tina was trying to get her non-profit off the ground and Joe was prosecuting some small cases for the US Attorney's office. He caught the attention of his supervisors for his meticulous preparation and was rewarded with much bigger and more complex cases. Tina made it through her first summer camp and was walking on air the rest of the year. The camp was only a week long back then and only 20 girls signed up. In fact, Joe and Tina had to dip into their meager savings to make it happen that first year, but Joe melted whenever he saw the devastated look on Tina's face when she had to settle for something less than what she really wanted.

After they passed their two-year anniversary and officially wrapped up their newlywed phase, they bought their first and only house. Joe got a raise and Tina was able to charm a few attorneys at a large Mergers and Acquisitions firm into fully sponsoring her camp and they began to live like a real married couple. They decided to try for a baby, but it was taking longer than they thought it should. A few trips to the gynecologist revealed that Tina suffered from endometriosis, a condition where the tissue grows outside of the uterus. The OB/GYN broke the news that Tina was incapable of conceiving. They were caught completely off guard, as Tina never showed any signs of a problem. The physician was soothing and answered all their questions, but was sure to offer no hope that she would ever have a child. Devastated, they went home in a daze and collapsed on the sofa. Tina broke down and cried and Joe tried to offer some measure of reassurance, but a dark cloud settled over Tina that did not truly lift for several months, until she began to prepare for the next summer camp.

Things gradually improved over the next few years. Tina's camp grew in numbers, Joe became something of a reliable prosecutor and even received another pay raise, and they were able to take a vacation in Boca Raton. Tina gradually accepted her condition and they even talked about adopting once or twice. Joe didn't press her, but he thought she seemed to perk up a bit when the topic came up. But something changed in Tina's mood over the last two years. Tina threw herself into her work, almost compulsively, and started dressing more professionally. She put forth more effort into fundraising than she had in the past and spent hours devouring spreadsheets and cost projections. One evening, Joe watched Tina work a room at a charity event and, to his amazement, she switched into a gear that he wasn't aware she had. She was positively radiant and bewitching to people that Joe and Tina usually didn't associate with. She exuded confidence when she talked to corporate presidents and captains of industry. She smiled warmly and would let her hand linger on their elbows, she even giggled when they told off-color jokes. She developed such a knack for charming Chicago's elite that she was invited to lunch with the Mayor of Chicago (along with a half-dozen other non-profit organizers, but still). She was rewarded for her efforts; the camp more than doubled in size and even got a small write-up in the Trib. Joe was happy that Tina was happy and she seemed to find fulfillment in their life together.

Joe snapped back to the drive and exited off the highway. He looked at himself in the rear-view mirror and decided that he still had quite a bit going for himself at 38 years old. So what if it took him a little longer to find what most people had in life? He and Tina had a great future ahead of them. Joe pulled into the parking garage and mentally prepared for another day at the office. He was looking forward to working on some new cases, anything that wasn't about Old Earl was an improvement.

Chapter 5

The weeks passed and Joe got back into a rhythm after losing Earl's case. He usually recovered from a loss more quickly, but Earl lingered in Joe's mind for some reason. Tina's schedule normalized, she didn't stay up working on the computer quite as late even though camp was rapidly approaching. Joe assumed Tina must have had the camp preparation clocked after enough years of operation and didn't need to work on the computer at home as much.

Joe had a few cases plead out in early June, and actually got some kudos from Washington when a defendant in an insider trading case accepted a plea bargain. Anthony Dilweg was a trader at the Chicago Mercantile Exchange. The "Merc" is a large financial and commodity exchange in Chicago, similar to the New York Stock Exchange. Dilweg was a senior commodities trader on the floor and after a decade of trading and a seven-figure annual income, he came up with an ingenious way of making so much money that it qualified in his mind as "obscene." Although many traders get caught up in exotic financial investment vehicles, the Merc is, at its heart, a commodities-based market. Meat, gold, produce, metals, pretty much anything that comes from a farm or a mine is traded there. Dilweg spent enough time on the floor that he discovered a simple pattern emerged: when the price of one class of Livestock moved more than ½ point in any direction, the other Livestock prices followed suit. Most rookie traders could figure out that much.

But Dilweg noticed that the swings were more gradual and that it took two consecutive ¼ point swings in, for example, feeder cattle, to cause the shift in lean hogs and, eventually, live cattle. Dilweg would watch for a ¼ point move in one class of livestock and buy options in the others.

To complete the trend, he just had to make sure the prices on the other two would climb as well. He would start by planting rumors about disruptions in the wheat and corn supply lines, perhaps by claiming Congress was about to eliminate agriculture subsidies or that there was a brewing labor dispute among members of a major Midwest farm co-op. Like clockwork, the price of Agriculture contracts would start to climb within an hour or two. And by threatening the food supply for the Livestock, the contracts on the Livestock became more valuable and the additional ¼ point swing became inevitable.

The Securities and Exchange Commission deals with people planting rumors every day. To combat the threat, the SEC simply monitors all transactions to see who purchased the affected stock in the days before the swing and *voila*, the rumor-monger is brought to justice. But because Dilweg never traded in wheat, corn or soy, he never showed up on the SEC's radar when they would review who made Agriculture purchases immediately before the swings occurred. Meanwhile, once the SEC, traders, and financial reporters could dispel the rumors about the Agriculture threats, the prices would fall again, usually within a few hours. But the Livestock prices took several days to normalize, more than enough time for Dilweg to exercise his options and fade back to anonymity. But Dilweg's plan imploded when he bragged about his foolproof method to his girlfriend, whom he subsequently infected with herpes and then dumped for a Venezuelan hand model. The ex-girlfriend dropped a dime to the SEC and Joe was assigned the criminal prosecution. Hell hath no fury like a woman scorned.

Despite hiring some of the most expensive white collar attorneys in Chicago, Joe crushed Dilweg in some pretrial motions and even with the significant legal resources available, Dilweg decided to plead out. Joe agreed to recommend 24 months in prison and to formally request the Bureau of Prisons allow Dilweg to serve his time at FCI-Ashland, Kentucky, in order to be close to his cousin. His "cousin" was more like his late cousin's bombshell of a wife who lived in South Charleston, West Virginia, over an hour from the prison. Joe knew Dilweg's desire had nothing to do with his cousin's widow, well, it had a little to do with her anyway. FCI-Ashland was named by Forbes magazine as one of the cushiest prisons in the entire federal system. But it was no skin off Joe's nose, Dilweg was a white collar criminal serving a relatively short sentence, and the amount of time and money his office would have to devote to the trial could easily approach a million dollars. With the constant budget crunch US Attorneys' offices were under nationwide, pleading out a case like this doesn't get Joe ink in the paper, but it might get him a promotion to Section head.

The US Attorney's Office is, for lack of a better description, Uncle Sam's law firm. The US Attorneys run the office and are appointed by the President, but the Assistant US Attorneys are non-political career hires. The Federal court system is divided up by Districts, generally corresponding to population. Illinois, for example, has three Federal Districts. The Northern District is comprised of the Eastern Division, which includes Chicago, and the Western Division, which includes Rockford. The Central District covers Peoria, Champaign and Springfield, and the Southern District handles whatever problems spill over into Illinois from St. Louis, Missouri. Each office is divided into a Criminal Division with multiple Sections (General Crimes, Narcotics and Gangs, National Security, Financial Crimes, and the Public Corruption and Organized Crime), and a Civil Division (Civil Rights, Environmental, Food and Drug, Civil Fraud, and Financial Litigation). Although Joe wasn't handling the sexy cases that drew headlines and face time on the national news like his colleagues prosecuting al Qaeda, Hell's Angels or even the mafia ("The Outfit," as it is known in Chicago), he considered his work just as important and he knew his fellow prosecutors considered Joe an important cog in the machine.

Joe had a new lawyer shadowing him during the Dilweg plea negotiations. His office hired an attractive attorney named Jacqueline Dekker from John Marshall Law School. Jackie was like most of the attorneys his office hired: young, eager to learn, top quarter of her class and idealistic. People like that gave the office youth and energy which kept it a fun place to work. She was a leggy blonde who played volleyball as an undergrad at Northwestern and was nearly six feet tall in heels. She wore her hair in a ponytail some days, but usually it was flowing around her shoulders. She occasionally wore black-rimmed glasses, which made her look smarter and, for some reason, even more striking. Joe wondered if she thought he was handsome (if he wasn't married, that is), and he was more than willing to show her the ropes. Jackie was technically assigned to the General Crimes Section, but she was really a floater, meaning she did a little work for each section until she found a home. Lately, she was splitting time assisting Joe on the Dilweg case and shadowing another prosecutor on a case involving a group of Eastern European gangsters trafficking young girls from Poland and the Ukraine.

After the Dilweg plea, Joe decided he earned an early trip home so he snuck out of the office a few minutes before 5:00 p.m. He arrived home the same time Tina did. She was a bit frazzled with the camp just two weeks away. He kissed her on the cheek and they walked in together.

"Joe, I lost my cell phone today, so I got a new one and have to give you the number."

"You lost it? Where? Golly, did you cancel the account?" Joe tended to get nervous when he lost something, but Tina seemed entirely unconcerned.

"Well, I didn't lose it so much as I dropped it down the toilet at the office and I really don't want it back. I went to the mall and set up the new account. Here, I am calling you with my new phone, so you'll have the new number and you can add it to your address book."

Joe's phone buzzed and he spent a few minutes fiddling with the keypad adding Tina's new number. *Did they give out new numbers when you lose your old phone?* It seemed odd, but the day's events in the Dilweg case overtook his thoughts and the cell phone issue quickly ran from his mind. They ate comfort food for dinner, garden salad and some leftover potato soup from the freezer.

Joe began gathering the dishes when Tina, apparently struck by an idea, quickstepped out of the room. She returned with a bag from a department store that Joe always considered a little pricey for his taste.

"Joe, look at what I picked up today!" Tina reached in and pulled out a large square package of bed sheets. "1,000 thread count Egyptian cotton. Aren't they luxurious?"

Joe reached out and held the package at arm's length like it was a dead rat. "Hmm. So you just went out and bought these?"

"Yeah, they are sooo nice. I read an article that said Demi Mo-"

Joe cut her off. "So, these were a bit on the expensive side?" Joe furrowed his brow as he twisted the bundle back and forth for a better look.

"Well, I mean, they weren't *that* expensive. They say that if you-"

Joe handed the sheets back to Tina. "Did you save the receipt?"

Tina gave an exaggerated frown and adopted a pouty expression. Joe paused and ultimately surrendered to her. "Oh, alright." Tina smiled warmly, threw her arms around his neck and gave him a kiss on the cheek before running upstairs.

They retired to their separate cocoons, Joe on the sofa with his headphones, Tina to her office. Joe worked for an hour and then decided to seek out Tina for some company. He walked into her office and paused as Tina sat transfixed with her headphones on watching a YouTube video of a ballerina. The dancer was dressed in white and glided effortlessly across the stage, illuminated by the footlights. It was clear to Joe that she was performing in some grand palace, no doubt in front of a packed audience watching her every move, rapt.

"She's graceful," Joe said.

Tina jumped and ripped off her headphones. "Oh! You frightened me! I didn't hear you come in."

"Oh, I'm sorry. Didn't mean to sneak up on you. I was bored and just wanted to say hello." Joe felt genuinely guilty about making Tina uncomfortable.

"It's fine, Joe." Tina turned back toward the monitor. "She is lovely, isn't she? Her name is Alessandra Ferri, she's an Italian prima ballerina and she is just the greatest. Look at her, isn't she gorgeous?"

"She is," Joe replied. He gave her a kiss and started to walk out. He returned to his cocoon but his mind was occupied. *Alessandra...Alessandra...what an unusual name. Where had I heard that before?*

Chapter 6

The next day, Wednesday, Joe was buried in a file working on a new fraud case. The lead FBI agent mucked up the case when he continued interviewing the suspect after the suspect asked some questions about hiring an attorney. Black letter law dictates the agent should have stopped the interrogation, advised the suspect that he really couldn't offer advice one way or the other, and then politely asked the suspect if he wanted to continue talking himself into a lengthy prison sentence (or, more appropriately, "assisting the investigation"). Otherwise, he would state that they could stop everything and the suspect would be allowed to consult with an attorney. Instead, the agent relayed a story about how his lawyer and his ex-wife's lawyer teamed up to screw the hell out of him in the divorce and that they were all a bunch of lousy shysters. Then he continued on with the interview and exacted a damning confession, which was now sure to be thrown out of court. It was a dumb mistake and Joe would have to remember this anecdote in the annual training that the prosecutors put on for federal law enforcement personnel. Joe decided he needed to talk to Suds Milder about the matter and left his office. He walked down the hall and paused when he saw Jackie glued to her computer screen.

"Hey rookie, sit any closer and you'll go blind," Joe said cheerfully.

"Oh, ummm, I'm sorry." Jackie was flushed and stammered a bit. She pushed back from her desk and revealed her blue skirt, now resting above her knee, and her sheer stockings. Joe followed them from her knees down to her not-quite stiletto heels, which she was nonchalantly trying to slip back on. *If I wasn't a married man, I would definitely ask her out on a date*, he thought.

"No worries. What has you so intense?" he asked.

34

"Well, I am working with Skinner on this Eastern Bloc trafficking case and, you know, these young girls are brought over by these employment agencies. They tell these girls they will be doing housecleaning in the US while they go to a public school in the neighborhood. They are told they'll learn English, get free room and board, receive a stipend for their work, and they'll see movie stars walking down the street. They get here and realize they are going to be prostitutes, but by then it's too late and they have no money to go back. So they start hooking for the agency to earn money for the plane ticket back, but the traffickers string them out on heroin and between the cost of the drugs and the traffickers' cut from what the Johns pay, they just never get out."

Joe had to break his gaze from her legs and look up at her face. He felt a temporary sense of panic when she seemed to catch him staring at her hemline, which she promptly adjusted. Joe soldiered on, despite being suddenly afflicted with a stammer. "Uh, ye-yeah. I, um, had a couple cases like that back when I was a floater, they stay with you. It's the eyes. Those pictures of the girls' eyes, glazed over from the drugs and empty from the street life. They haunt you." Joe decided that he enjoyed mentoring Jackie, perhaps one day she would remember him as fondly as he remembers Lou Jackson.

Jackie looked back at the screen. "Yeah, I can see that. I found a site where you select the girl you want and it shows you everything they are willing to do. And for how much. $50 gets you one thing, but $100 gets you everything else. Sick."

"Yeah If you want to chat about it or get some help, my door is always open," Joe said with an inviting smile.

"Oh, umm, yeah. I think I'll be fine." Jackie did a poor job of concealing her discomfort and Joe quickly realized his offer sounded a bit too much like a flirtation, which certainly wasn't his intention. Now, Joe was blushing and was more embarrassed than Jackie. He quickly muttered a "thanks" (what exactly he was thanking her for, he didn't know) and he practically sprinted from her office, silently cursing his wandering eyes.

Joe returned to his office, gathered himself and returned to his file. Jackie left him so flustered he forgot what he was supposed to ask his supervisor about. But he ruminated on the encounter and felt genuinely guilty that Jackie was forced to look at all the profiles of those poor women, and Joe decided he could review his old files for some tips to help her out. If he was going to mentor Jackie, after all, he needed to make sure she learned the most efficient way to work. He eagerly pulled up some old trafficking files to see what he could do to make Jackie's job easier.

The trafficking cases were always tough to crack. The employment agencies never used the same websites. Instead, they used multiple sites and closed them down after a month and migrated to new sites and new servers. They drifted in and out of internet chat rooms and emailed old customers directly about new girls for the customers to sample. Law enforcement could always find one girl here and there, but to really pique the interest of the Federal government, you needed to tie all the girls together with the traffickers, the international travel, and the money distribution. Without the entire network, it was just a local case of "girl sleeps with guy for $100," which the Chicago PD understandably feels is far from the most pressing issue they face on any given day. Cases take an eternity to build and because the undercover agents cannot exactly sleep with the women first, the arrests are one at a time, most of the girls don't talk other than to give a false name, and they quickly bail out for $50. Then they disappear back to Eastern Europe, are moved to another city to start work, or have a convenient overdose in an alley somewhere and the case sits on a shelf in perpetuity.

Joe opened some of the old websites to see if they were still active. Most corporate offices in the US have an IT Department that track all the websites employees visit and block the high-risk and pornographic ones, while sending an auto-alert to the host announcing the employee's transgression. But because the Dirksen Federal Building hosts the US Marshal's office in addition to the US Attorney's office, the users routinely deal with cases of child pornography, internet fraud, online gambling and interstate prostitution. The IT Department intentionally designed the firewall to block viruses, not content. Web histories and cookies are automatically deleted after 24 hours in a new effort to conserve server space, which conserves money. So any prosecutor in the office can access a normally illegal site without having to constantly call IT to turn off the filter or explain to their supervisor why they had to spend all month visiting offshore online poker sites.

Joe clicked link after link, but they were all dead and he kept getting host error messages. He was about to give up when one link connected him to an active site. Joe spent a few minutes looking at the home page listing several "escorts." But the page for each linked to a Craigslist ad, which had expired. Another dead end. He opened Craigslist and entered some basic search terms in the personal services section, "Chicago" and "escort" seemed to do the trick, but the first few ads were all an invitation to another link that appeared to be spam, so he gave up on that. He made a mental note to tell Jackie to avoid the Craigslist ads, she would probably appreciate the tip. He scrolled down to a post about high-end "outcalls," meaning the escorts would go to the Johns' house or hotel room. The gangs favored the use of outcalls because the cops would not be able to tie the gang to one of its safe houses or a stolen credit card used for a hotel reservation. And if they were lucky, they would find a house worth robbing after the John got tired of the girl (and if the John has an inkling who the thieves were, it's unlikely he would call the police anyway). The only risk was sending the girl to a dangerous house, but a dead hooker wasn't anything an Eastern European white slave trader would lose any sleep over. Joe decided the term "outcall" was a good one to teach Jackie.

He clicked the "outcall" link for Chicago high-end escorts and a page opened. It was a white background with soft pink lettering, billing itself as "Provocateur Courtesans." He realized quickly that this was a professional set-up with a lot of effort spent developing the site, far from the slap-dash website templates the low-end hustlers used. It looked new, the host probably bought the domain name from a defunct site. There were a number of tabs: *About Us – Privacy Policy – Contacts – Our Girls – Customer Reviews*. Joe clicked "About Us" and a page popped up with several paragraphs written in proper English (a sure sign someone with an education spent time editing the page), assuring the visitor that their "courtesans" were the classiest and most sophisticated women in the world. The *Privacy Policy* tab assured the visitor that customer information is never retained and that information is never disclosed to any "third party." That meant Joe and his pals. *Contacts* was a link where customers were given the escort's particular instructions: "Never call Mindy after 5:00 p.m., No texting Sarah, Leave a message for Brittney-she won't answer if you call," and the like. The visitor clicks a tab to send an anonymous email with some basic information, and the site promises the escort's phone number will be emailed back and the customer could close the loop directly with the escort.

Joe took a breath, clicked the *Our Girls* tab, and steeled himself for the haunting photos he was used to seeing. The computer spent nearly half a minute loading the page and rendering the photos. Joe realized this was no low-end operation. The page loaded and Joe was greeted by a full page of thumbnail pictures. He clicked the first thumbnail on the list and was greeted with a selection of high-resolution pictures. The photographs were all carefully staged and the sets appeared to be from photoshoots in professional photography studios, as opposed to some cheap hotel room. Although the faces were obscured by the model's arm or were blurred out completely, Joe could tell the half-naked women maintained themselves quite well. The first model had muscle tone and a healthy figure and appeared to be wearing expensive lingerie and jewelry. He clicked the back arrow and then clicked the next group of photographs on the list. The same kind of professional portfolio appeared for the next escort who had the same kind of muscular, lean figure.

At first, Joe thought it was a scam. Some traffickers use pictures of celebrities or Victoria Secret models to reel in the John and then stick him with a waif, strung out and skinny (and frankly, if a customer was dumb enough to think he was renting Angelina Jolie for $75 per hour, he deserved the venereal disease he was sure to contract). But Joe saw the price chart at the top of the page and knew it was no bait-and-switch: Two hour minimum: $1,500. Overnight: $2,500. Weekend (Friday 5:00 p.m. through Sunday 7:00 p.m.): $5,000. This was no Eastern European gang, this was something else entirely. Joe began reading through the profiles: "Natasha" is a physician in central Illinois who did some modeling in medical school; "Rachel" is an astrophysicist in a private college in the upper Midwest and is a part-time Pilates instructor; "Laura" is the vice president of a financial services company in suburban Chicago and loving wife; "Catherine" is a housewife, soccer-mom of three and a competitive triathlete. Joe was shocked. He had never seen women like this - smart, professional, successful and physically perfect. Why were they doing this? They clearly didn't need the money. It had to be a scam.

Joe was about to log off when he saw a name that sucked the air from his lungs: *Alessandra.* He stared at the name for a moment while his mind processed what he was seeing. *Alessandra. The name of the ballerina from the video. The name from the…from the…where did I see it before? The text. The text on Tina's phone. Uh oh.* He started to lose focus, the words became blurry. Joe grabbed the sides of the desk tightly and took a deep breath. *It is a coincidence. Breathe. Click the link, it's not her.* Joe gathered himself and hovered the mouse arrow over the thumbnail. It only showed the back of a woman's head, but the hair color looked different. Joe hesitated before clicking the mouse, looked around, and got up to close the door to his office. He tried to look casual but did a poor job. But because Joe was often overlooked in the office, no one paid him any mind. Joe sat back down and took another deep breath. He pointed the mouse over the thumbnail and clicked the link. The page started to load and seemed to freeze. *What was the problem? It shouldn't take this long. Did the site crash?* He considered shutting down and restarting when the hi-res pictures began to load. The page opened and showed a petite girl with dishwater blonde hair and a toned figure. The woman's hair was shorter than Tina's, but then again Tina did wear it short the year before. There were four pictures and all of them were from the back. Joe didn't recognize the room, and the model wore generic panties that offered no clue as to her identity. He had seen his wife naked a thousand times but couldn't be sure if it was her. Joe quickly analyzed the picture for confirmation that it couldn't be her. A tattoo, a birthmark, a scar, anything. *Could they have been airbrushed out?* That made the most sense. Seeing no clear evidence one way or the other he read the bio: *Hi all! My name is Alessandra. I run my own small business and travel to Europe quite a bit for work. I gave up a career in dance and now I want to give you a private show! I promise you will NOT be disappointed. Check out my menu and hit me up!*

Joe couldn't concentrate, too much was running through his mind. *It couldn't be her, Tina has a non-profit, she doesn't really "run her own small business." Tina travels only rarely, and then only to Wisconsin, she has never been to Europe. She did give up dancing, but that was more like a college major than a career. She never said "hit me up" in her life, that doesn't sound like something she'd say. Although the site operators probably edit the bios, so maybe someone else added that.*

39

Joe started to get a pounding headache and he needed to get out of there. He closed the webpage and made sure he deleted his browsing history, just to be safe. He shut down the computer and walked to the door. He passed Ellen and told her that he caught a bug and needed to head home and take something for it. She asked if he was going to return before 5:00 p.m. or simply remain home for the afternoon. Joe couldn't deal with Ellen at the moment and simply muttered "I don't know, whatever," and headed for the elevator.

Chapter 7

Joe was in a fog and couldn't remember the drive home. He parked in the garage, shut off the engine and sat in silence for what felt like an eternity. He lumbered inside and saw it was only 3:00 p.m., a couple hours before Tina would come home from the office. Joe collapsed on the sofa and tried to process the events of the afternoon. His head began to clear and he realized it had to be a misunderstanding. Tina's hair was short once, but that was almost two years ago. And she's never been to Europe. And he was being silly. He began to feel more relaxed and shook his head as he considered the folly of it all. Joe marched upstairs, changed clothes and walked back down the hall past Tina's office. He paused and peered inside. *She took her laptop with her, but it was password protected anyway. And what the heck am I thinking? I'm not going to spy on my wife. That's what suspicious husbands do.*

He began preparing dinner and uncorked a bottle of wine when Tina came home. She appeared to be genuinely surprised to see him home so early, and gave him a kiss.

"What are you doing home at this time of day?" she asked.

Joe smiled and gave Tina a lingering hug. "I wasn't feeling too hot and left early. Feeling better now, though."

Tina put her hand on his forehead and declared him normal. All the same, she said, he was pale and she ordered him to the sofa while she finished cooking. He settled in with a blanket and started to feel better. Tina brought him dinner and they carefully ate on the sofa. They each talked about their day and Joe felt more cared for than he had in weeks. Tina gathered the dishes and said she needed to get some work done and ordered Joe to watch some tv or get some sleep, but no computer was allowed. Tina scampered upstairs and Joe closed his eyes and tried to drift off to sleep. He was awakened after a half hour when the phone in his pocket chirped. Joe pulled it out and was greeted with a text telling him that AT&T could save him money over his current data plan. He deleted the text and slipped the phone back in his pocket. He lay back down and was struck with a thought. *What was that text Tina got the month before? Something about an appointment. It said the name "Alessandra".*

Joe couldn't chase the thought out of his head. He was awake now, and he knew he needed to kill this idea before he could get anything resembling a good night's sleep. He thought about the phone. Tina lost her phone and bought a new one. *Did she really lose it? She said she lost it down the toilet at work. How did she manage to do that, exactly?* He thought about cases his office prosecuted involving drug dealers who constantly change phones and contact numbers to avoid detection. *Couldn't she keep the old number on the new phone?* Joe was no technological wizard and didn't know how that worked. *The phone companies must have a policy about that. Maybe transferring an old number was an extra fee or something.* Tina hated contracts and convinced Joe that prepaid phones, loaded monthly with a fixed number of minutes, was the best option. Joe always gave Tina permission to handle all of that. Did he have her old number? He checked his phone but her new number was in his address book. *Dead end. Wait, I have the phone's call history. Tina called me the day before she lost the phone, but that was a month ago. Did the phone keep the call history that long?* He checked, *nope, they auto-deleted after a week. Wait, Tina emailed me her new number when she got the phone the previous summer.* He pulled out his laptop and checked his email history. The inbox was nearly empty. *Another dead end. Wait, I sent her a reply email confirming that I had the new number.* He checked the outbox and searched...*eureka!* Joe scanned the email and located the original number. He had to slow down his breathing and listened for Tina, she was still upstairs.

Joe contemplated his next move. He needed to be sure. He couldn't use his own phone, she would know it was him. He had to think. He needed a phone. Could this wait until tomorrow? No, it couldn't, he needed to know *now.* Joe got up from the couch and climbed the stairs. He endeavored to make as much noise as possible and he eased open the door to Tina's office, tapping on the doorjamb. She looked up, greeted him with a big smile and asked how he was feeling.

42

"Much better. I am going to run out to grab some Nyquil. Be back in a few."

"Honey, you should rest. I am sure we have something here you can take."

"No, that's fine. You can keep surfing the internet, I'll be back in a half hour or so." The mention of surfing the web undisturbed must have appealed to Tina, because she suddenly changed her tune.

"Well, if you really need Nyquil, maybe you should go."

Joe's suspicions were again raised, and for the moment he knew he was doing the right thing to alleviate his doubts. Joe waved goodbye, explaining to Tina that he didn't want to kiss her and get her sick, although he couldn't quite bring himself to kiss her at that moment anyway.

Joe grabbed his wallet and keys and climbed into the car. He pulled out of the driveway and headed for a strip mall a few miles away. He kept thinking how crazy this all was. *What am I doing? Driving to some strip mall cell phone store at 7:00 p.m. at night. Normal husbands don't do this.* In spite of the debate in his head, Joe soldiered on and after 15 minutes he pulled into the store's parking lot. He straightened up and walked in and immediately felt the clerk's eyes boring into his back as if Joe was a cop looking to bust the place. The clerk was a squat African American man wearing a football jersey of some sort, some college that Joe never heard of. He had cornrows braided tight against his head and Joe decided he looked like someone he might end up prosecuting one day. Joe had a measure of contempt for this person he never met, largely due to his own foul mood. He didn't like this darkness that surrounded him, and he committed himself to getting through this foolishness and back to some semblance of normalcy.

The clerk piped up. "Can I help you, man?"

Joe looked at him sternly. "I need a cell phone, I will prepay for a month. I don't want a plan."

The clerk eyed him up and down and asked, "Is this charge?"

"Cash," Joe said as he reached in his pocket and peeled off $200. The clerk smiled, revealing a gold tooth, and reached behind the counter.

"We got a couple kinds fo' you," he said.

"I don't care, just something basic. How long is this going to take?"

The clerk looked at Joe with a degree of suspicion, but his demeanor quickly gave way to a knowing smile. Joe hated him at that instant.

"I got ya, man. This one here's refurbished but it's pretty good. $100 for the phone and $40 for the first two months of data. After that, you can reload minutes. No i.d. needed for this one. You can take it and bounce."

"Can I text?" Joe asked.

"Oh yeah, but you can only surf the web for, like, five hours or somethin' before you start paying golden time."

"That's fine." Joe paid the clerk and left. The clerk didn't bother to offer a receipt. Joe sat in the parking lot and turned the phone on. He gave himself a quick tutorial, put the car in gear and headed home. He passed the Walgreens and nearly caused an accident when he hit the brakes. *Nyquil.* He turned into the parking lot, ran inside and picked up a bottle and headed back home. He pulled into the garage and sat for a moment while he constructed an alibi for his extended trip to a pharmacy located just a few blocks away.

Tina called down to him, "Hon, you home?"

"Yeah, I'll be up in a few," he said. Joe took note that she didn't come down to check on him or ask why he was gone for so long, instead she stayed on her computer. Joe was genuinely angry now and wasn't quite sure what to do with himself. He kicked off his shoes and lay on the sofa under a blanket. He pulled out his laptop, opened his email account and put Tina's old number in the text feature of the new phone. He began to type, deleted a few drafts, and then settled on the script.

His finger hovered over the keypad for a few minutes while his heart raced. He took a deep breath and pressed "send." He waited. Nothing happened. Minutes went by, still nothing. He kept checking the phone, still nothing. He took a large drink of Nyquil and stashed the phone in the back of the desk drawer. He wandered upstairs, quietly this time, and found Tina sitting at the computer with her headphones on, working on some kind of a document. He could make out the word "insurance" and concluded it was truly related to the camp. He put on his pajamas and crawled into bed. The Nyquil did its job and he was fast asleep within minutes. He dreamt of Earl again, sneering at him. This time Earl was sitting across from Joe in his office. He couldn't make out what Earl was saying, but the look of contempt was unmistakable. Joe looked at the door and saw Jackie walk past, she gave him a slight smile and continued on. Earl was mumbling louder but Joe couldn't make it out. Joe began yelling at Earl, "Be quiet! Be quiet!" Joe woke with a start as the sunlight pierced the bedroom windows. He slept the whole night. Tina was already up and dressed, Joe stumbled out of bed and made his way to the bathroom as Tina finished brushing her teeth.

"Wow, you were really out last night," she said.

"Yeah, that Nyquil did me in." Joe managed to get showered and dressed and went to the kitchen. Tina was already getting in her car. Joe went to the living room and grabbed his wallet, keys and cell phone. He paused, turned and ran to the living room and rifled through the desk. *New phone…the text!* Until that moment Joe forgot about the text. He checked the phone and there was no response. He sighed, deciding he was being foolish. Tina didn't text him, or Alessandra didn't, so it must have been fine. *Besides, where would Tina keep the phone? She lost it at work. Work? Did she keep it at work?* Joe's mind raced and he dashed to his car. He peeled out of the driveway, turned down Tina's usual route and spied her car at a stop light a block ahead. Joe followed slowly and kept his distance. The drive seemed to take forever and Joe argued with himself the entire time as to whether these were the acts of a worried man or completely irrational husband. *I'm really looking out for her. We need to satisfy ourselves about this nonsense so we can go on with our lives*, Joe told himself.

After 15 minutes of Joe's amateur efforts to tail Tina without being noticed, she finally pulled into the parking lot of her office complex. Tina rented a small office in a series of cookie-cutter buildings. Joe helped her negotiate the lease and was rather proud of his efforts. The buildings featured a number of doctors and insurance agents, and more than a few lawyers. Joe drove around the block as she parked and got out of the car. Tina gave no hint that she was aware Joe was following her and she walked into the building. Joe parked across the street, pulled out the new cell phone and waited. *A minute to get in the office, a minute to turn on the light and computer, a minute to check the phone.* The minutes seemed like hours as Joe waited for a response. He reviewed the text he sent the night before: *Alessandra, are you free tonight? I would like to book an appointment.* Joe knew Tina would be home by 5:00 p.m., but tomorrow night, Friday, there was some kind of

45

function at an insurance company's office that she had to go to in order to raise a few dollars for the summer camp, just two weeks away. He stared at the phone and waited. He was starting to feel sick again. His palms were sweating and after ten minutes, Joe gave up and decided he needed to go to work. He opened his sport coat to stash the phone inside when it jumped in his hand, vibrating to announce a new text. Joe purchased the phone 12 hours earlier, it was no spam or wrong number. Joe only texted one number, Tina's old phone. He swallowed hard and opened the phone, a text stared back at him: *Not tonight, sorry. :(But I will be available for an appointment tomorrow, from 5:00 p.m.-7:00 p.m. Outcall only! Hit me up if you are interested. — Alessandra.*

Chapter 8

Joe shut off the phone and dropped it in his jacket pocket. He unbuckled the seat belt, opened the car door, leaned out, and threw up on the pavement. He closed the door and sat motionless, struggling to detach himself from the moment. He started the car, put it in gear, and drove to work. *I can't miss another day, everyone will suspect that I just learned my wife was a professional hooker. It will be plain as day. Why else would I miss work?*

Joe was on autopilot the entire trip and struggled to form a coherent thought in his head. He arrived at the office, half expecting to be greeted by a mixture of sympathy and judgment from his coworkers, as if they could deduce the entire sordid tale from his facial expression. Joe simply nodded to Ellen as he entered the lobby, she gave an overly cheery 'good morning,' even for Ellen. At that moment, Joe wanted to punch her stupid civil-service face. He walked to his office, closed the door, and sat down at the computer. Without thinking, he opened the files he reviewed the day before and clicked the same series of links until he arrived at Alessandra's profile. Looking through a new lens, the picture came into focus: *of course it was Tina.* The woman's figure, the backstory, everything. It was her. God, he hated her so. He looked at the profile much closer now, and focused on the matrix at the bottom of the page that explained the courtesan's limits. Joe deduced that each girl submitted responses to a questionnaire with a few dozen boxes and checked the boxes that correspond to the acts they were willing to perform. "Alessandra" checked a number of boxes. Quite a lot of them, actually. Joe could grasp what most of them meant: *oral-giving (to completion), oral-receiving, females, multiple partners-couples, multiple partners-males (2), single females, Greek, bareback (verified clients only), GFE.* Joe knew what the first two meant, completion meant orgasm and he surmised the next three meant she would engage women and couples, either man-woman or two men. He could make an educated guess what *Greek* meant. He recalled from a movie he saw years ago that bareback meant sex without a condom, he assumed *verified* meant she at least needed to know the Johns were disease/drug free before she agreed to that, and *GFE*.

Joe scanned some of the trafficking intelligence files he had in his computer to find the glossary of terms common to the sex trade. He located the description and felt a wave of nausea as he read: *GFE – Girl Friend Experience. Generally implies a session that is more akin to lovemaking with a girlfriend than sex with a prostitute. May include sharing personal stories, goals, dreams, and other intimate thoughts. May also include DFK (Deep French Kissing).* Joe knew prostitutes never allowed French kissing, it was considered too intimate an act and was the one thing a prostitute would keep to herself, something that no customer could have. Joe considered the last two: *Tina would have sex with her clients, without a condom, and then come home and have sex with me. She would also kiss these men, on the mouth, and then come home and kiss me, with the same mouth.* Joe struggled with which act of the final two offended him more. Both were intimate in their own way, but he decided the GFE was the ultimate betrayal of the bonds of marriage.

Joe calmly closed all the webpages and walked out of his office. Ellen looked up from her monitor, did a double-take and blurted out, "Whoa, you feeling alright Joe? Heavens, you look like a sheet."

"Yeah, bug from yesterday, just need a minute and some water." Joe quickstepped to the bathroom and threw up again. He splashed some water on his face and decided what to do next. *Think, Joe. Think. What the hell do I do now? Call her? No. No way.*

Joe went back to his office, word must have gotten around because others were now eyeing him warily. He made it to his office, closed the door and sat down. He thumbed through his rolodex and dialed a number.

"Family medical, how can I help you," the voice on the other end asked.

"This is Joe Haise, can I get in to see Doctor Phillips? It's important."

"Aww, got the flu bug? It's going around. We had a cancellation, can you be here in an hour?"

"I'll be there." Joe hung up and bolted for his car, telling Ellen he had a doctor's appointment as he rushed past her desk. She told him to take care of himself, but never bothered to look up from her computer. Empathy was not actually a requirement of her job, so she probably assumed she was going above and beyond the call by telling Joe to take care of himself.

Joe peeled out of the parking garage and made it to the doctor's office in plenty of time. He checked in and was given a surgical mask, the intake nurse took one look and pronounced that he had the flu. Joe was escorted to the back, weighed and ushered to an exam room. He complained about feeling flu-ish, and the nurse dutifully took his vitals, noted his symptoms in the chart and told Joe the doctor would be in shortly.

The grandfatherly Dr. Phillips appeared after a few minutes and greeted Joe with that sweet smile all family doctors have. "So, we have the flu, do we?"

Joe's face began to turn red, he swallowed hard and struggled to maintain a steady tone of voice. "Dr. Phillips, I need you to check me for STDs."

One thing Joe always liked about Tom Phillips, he was unflappable. He was probably a world-class poker player in another life. When Joe, his patient for the last 10 years and who has been with the same woman for more than seven years said he needed to be checked for STDs, Tom Phillips did not so much as raise an eyebrow.

"I see. Are you worried about HIV? Coupled with your flu symptoms, I think I have some real concerns here."

"No," Joe said. "I am just a little nervous today Tom, I don't have the flu. I need to be checked for HIV, herpes, Chlamydia. Whatever. I just need some kind of reassurance."

Tom made a few notes in the chart and addressed Joe without ever looking up from the page, probably assuming that avoiding eye contact will bring more honest information. "Joe, are you engaging in unsafe or risky behavior?"

"Me?! No. God, no. I haven't, you know, done anything. *I'm* not the one who, ah, you know, does that sort of thing."

Tom Phillips heard the concern in Joe's voice and did not miss a

49

beat. "Hmm, I see. We'll run some tests, and I'll take a look for anything out of the ordinary. Can you lower your pants, please?" The physician gave a brief look, declared Joe in good health from the outside, and ordered some lab work.

"Nancy will come back in and will take you down the hall for a blood draw and urine sample. I will put a rush on it and get your results back in 24 hours. Now, if the results are positive for HIV, we will have to confirm, which will take a few more days. Until then, I will write you a prescription for some valium. You need to control your anxiety level until tomorrow when I can get the results back."

Joe felt better already, Tom really knew his audience and his reassuring tone had the intended effect. Joe shook his hand and was quickly ushered to the lab for blood and urine samples. Joe pocketed the prescription from the nurse and drove straight to the Walgreens down the street from his house. He waited for the prescription to be filled, paid and left. He sat in the car and scanned the instructions on the side of the bottle. Joe popped a valium and started the car. He wanted to take two, but he was a lightweight with wine and thought better of it. He drove home and changed clothes, looked in the fridge for lunch, then decided he couldn't eat. He sat on the couch, flipped on the television and channel surfed for a while when the valium hit him like a Peterbilt. He managed to lie down and, despite his double vision, pulled a blanket over himself and passed out.

Chapter 9

The valium impacted Joe more than he expected, he had a few dreams but they made no sense. He saw people with contorted faces and tried to talk to them, but he couldn't stand still long enough, he kept floating past them like an untethered balloon. He started to wake up in the late afternoon and tried to clear the fog from his head. He heard some noise as Tina called his name from the kitchen.

"Joe? I saw your car in the garage, are you sick again?"

Joe propped himself up and rubbed his eyes. He saw Tina's face and immediately imagined *Alessandra*. He couldn't look her in the eye and he felt a wave of contempt wash over him. "Not too well."

"You're not feeling too well? You look pale, I'll get you some tea. What flavor do you want?"

Joe was starting to lose focus, so he quickly lay back down and closed his eyes. He had to concentrate. "I don't know, whatever is fine. I need to close my eyes for a bit."

Tina retreated to the kitchen while Joe tried to decide what to say. What to say? Ann Landers never covered this one in her column, of that he was sure. *"Honey, I saw the darndest thing on the internet today." "Honey, since we're married, do you think I can get the GFE on a discount?" "Honey, I know Jesus consorted with whores, but he was a hell of a lot better sport than I am."*

Joe peered out from the blankets and saw Tina still standing in the kitchen. He couldn't deal with this right now. Not now. He sat up, reached for the valium, popped another tablet and chased it with a nearby glass of water. He put the bottle in his pocket so Tina wouldn't see what he was taking. He settled back under the blankets.

She brought the tea in and asked Joe if he needed anything. "No, just some rest. I don't want to get you sick."

Tina kissed the top of his head and headed upstairs. Joe pushed the blanket down with his feet and stared at the ceiling. He considered his options, breaking down the situation like one of his cases. He could confront her now, but then the cat is out of the bag. If she spent any of her earnings from the escort service on their mortgage, groceries, anything, they both could be charged with failing to report income on their tax returns. He could possibly still keep his law license, but he would certainly lose his job. A federal prosecutor whose wife was a hooker? No one would believe he had no idea what his wife was doing; they would conclude he is complicit, which is bad, or that he is a moron, which is probably worse. No, turning this into a public spectacle was a non-starter. Could he confront her privately and ask for a quickie divorce? He would have to submit sworn financial statements and testify in Cook County court during the divorce, and he would be forced to either commit perjury or confess to his wife's criminal activity. Nope, that was not on the menu. And to top it off, Tina's extracurriculars could come back to haunt Joe at any time if an old email suddenly surfaced or if the escort service got busted. The owner would likely cut a deal by exposing all the escorts and their clients and then Joe's divorce filings and tax returns would be front and center in the investigation. The statute of limitations on the living hell this could cause Joe is about 500 years.

Could I confront her, forgive her, and move on? Joe gave this the most thought. Maybe she was doing this to fund the camp so Joe would never have to dip into their savings like he did that first year, and her devotion to those poor girls ultimately clouded her judgment. But they didn't need the money for themselves, their household finances were in proper order. And even if Tina stopped fundraising altogether, the camp had more than enough cash in reserve for another five years of operation. No, she was doing this for some other reason.

Maybe she was sick or had some kind of psychological disorder. Maybe she hated doing this and was too ashamed to ask Joe for help. But women in this line of work usually display signs of desperation and go out of their way to let someone, *anyone*, know they want out. Tina went out of her way to keep Joe in the dark. In Joe's experience dealing with the criminal mind, people who were truly sick weren't all that clever. And Tina was very clever.

God, did she truly enjoy what she was doing? Joe shook off the debate raging in his head. Whatever her reasons, Joe wasn't sure he could stay married to her after what she'd done. After what he'd seen on the website. For the rest of his life he would look at her face and think about all the men she kissed with that mouth, all the men she slept with, the women, the couples. No, he could never un-see that.

Joe tossed and turned on the sofa realizing his life, as he knew it, as he *planned* it, was over. No adopting a child, no Tina by his side as he advanced through the ranks at the US Attorney's Office. He couldn't imagine ever making love to her again, not after imagining every disgusting, vile thing she did for money. How could he? Every urge in his body told him to get up, storm into her little office and confront her. His brain, however, said to wait. Joe wished he didn't think like a lawyer all the time, but he couldn't just turn it off. He was unable to conceptually distinguish the effect this information would have on his career from how it would impact the rest of his life. Joe pondered what his role in her choices could have been. *Did I drive her to this? How could I be in any way responsible for this situation? I get a steady paycheck each week and always tried to look good for her. Sure, my weight isn't always the best and the troops that comprise my hairline have been in retreat for the last year or two, but why would that matter? Love is supposed to conquer all that. I never stayed out late and never came home drunk. I never got a tattoo and we are always home, safe and sound, every night. I gave her a stable, predictable life with an established daily routine. Isn't that what a husband is supposed to provide a wife? No, this is all on her. I gave her everything I am supposed to as a husband, what else could she possibly want?*

Joe decided that every option was bad, but a few were worse than others. Anything that suggested the loss of his standing in the legal community was quickly dismissed, which left him to contemplate either a hush-hush divorce and a prayer that the truth will never get out, or a reconciliation and they simply pick up where they left off. *I am going to have to decide which option would be best for both of us, and then confront Tina once I solved the problem. Yes, that would work just fine. Now that the procedure was worked out, the substance was the thing. What am I supposed to do to with this debacle of a marriage?*

The valium kicked in before Joe could pare down his options any further and he passed out once again.

Joe woke in the middle of the night, still on the sofa. He took a minute to get his bearings, recalled what brought him to sleep on the sofa, and slumped back down. He grabbed his phone off the coffee table, it read 1:00 a.m. He stood up and used the powder room off the kitchen, splashed some water on his face and returned to living room. He looked up the stairs and was sure he saw a flicker of light from the hallway. He surmised Tina was on her computer again. *Wonder who she was preparing to "date" next?* Joe began to replay *Alessandra's* profile page from the website in his mind. The pictures, the bio, everything. It made him angry. He began to take inventory of all of his options again. In every case he prosecuted, Joe exhibited meticulous preparation. Sure, he misread juries from time to time, maybe underestimated his opponent once or twice, but he never let a detail escape his attention. That was his strength. He needed more information in order to make an informed decision. *Who were her clients? How often did she meet them?* He pulled out his laptop and opened his web browser. He shifted his position to be able to see Tina if she came down the stairs. He opened Google and began to type some search terms: "Alessandra," "escort" and "Chicago." He hovered the cursor over the search button and paused. He heard Tina rustling upstairs. He waited until she settled and he returned his attention to the laptop. He was about to hit the return button, but he hesitated. *Wait, what if the IRS seizes the laptop for unpaid taxes, or if the Chicago PD busts the escort operation? I can't play dumb if they check my search history and see what I did.* Joe carefully deleted the terms and reentered "Chicago Cubs bullpen" and hit enter. He breathed a sigh of relief as a few million hits returned.

Well, I can't do anything here, he thought. *Wait, I already loaded the escort pages at the office. But that's on a 24 hour auto-delete. I'm clear.* Joe needed to do his research at the office. How could he get more information on Tina's little hobby? He knew about keystroke logging software, basically a program the user loads onto a target's computer that enables the principal to monitor everything they do, websites they visited, passwords, chat logs, everything. Joe helped a few FBI agents obtain warrants to install similar programs on the computers of some book-making suspects. Civilians could pick up the software pretty much anywhere, Joe knew a few software stores in Kenosha, Wisconsin, about 45 minutes north of their house.

He also needed to know where Tina went at night, the routes she took, whether she had a hotel room she used. If "Alessandra" did outcall, she would travel to the John's locations, although presumably she would meet new customers at a neutral location to make sure they checked out. Joe also knew that agents used GPS devices to track a suspect's movements, but he did not really know how they worked. He knew there were GPS tracking devices he could buy in a tech store, but many were passive devices, meaning they stored the data on the device and could tell the principal where the target has been after removing the tracker's data card. But learning where Tina went long after a client defiled her did not really solve Joe's problem. He would need real-time data and he hoped he could get a real-time interactive device, but he didn't know whether that was available to civilians.

Do I need a hidden camera? And if I bought one, where would I install it? And even if I did install it, like a John's house, how would I get it in there? And how would I get it out? And could I stand to watch whatever the video captured? He needed to put this one on the back burner. He could get the other items up and running in short order, but the camera was a much more labor-intensive undertaking. He decided to wait on that one.

Joe put away the laptop and settled back in, but he found himself unable to sleep the rest of the night. Too much ran through his mind: their courtship, the wedding, their plans for the future. Joe gave up trying to sleep and stared at the ceiling until the sun began to rise and he got up from the sofa. He tiptoed upstairs, slipped into the guest bath and pulled a towel from under the sink. He took a quick shower, toweled off, and tiptoed back down the hall to the master bedroom, trying not to make the floor creak as he crept along. He eased open the bedroom door and looked at the rumpled heap on the bed, Tina didn't move. Joe crept into the closet, selected his clothes for the day and turned to leave. He paused and stared at Tina's face, partially buried underneath the covers. He became angry again. *She threw it all away, their life, everything, for what? To fulfill some twisted dream of becoming a common, disease-riddled harlot?* Joe decided she could pick out her own clothes for once. He turned and slipped out.

Joe finished dressing downstairs, adjusted his bow tie one last time, and grabbed a leftover muffin from the fridge. He scribbled a note for Tina, "Got up early and headed to the office, feeling better!" He read it and decided it was too positive, and rewrote it without the exclamation point and shoved the first note in his pocket. He grabbed his keys and wallet, and pulled the other cell phone from the back of the desk drawer. "Alessandra" didn't text him again. He stuffed the items in his pocket and headed out the door.

Chapter 10

Friday morning traffic was light and Joe arrived at the office before anyone else. He retreated to his office, closed the door and fired up the computer. He loaded the archived files from the prior investigation, followed the links, and again loaded the "Provocateur Courtesans" website. Joe didn't feel the same surge of anger as before, he was more detached this time, more clinical. Joe loaded *Alessandra's* page and realized he missed something from last time he visited the site, the tab for *Reviews*. He moved the cursor to the top of the page and clicked the tab. A new page loaded and it had each escort's name in bright blue lettering, attached to a hyperlink. Joe quickly found "Alessandra's" name and clicked the link. A new page loaded, white with soft pink lettering and a number of block quotes. Joe began to read. *"Alessandra is awesome! Petite body, but a bundle of dynamite in bed! Worth every penny. – Gary M." "Alessandra cost quite a bit for the weekend, but my wife and I were left totally satisfied. She took as much time with her as with me, and let's just say she did everything she said she would do on her profile page. And I mean EVERYTHING. - Bob and Susan J." "Alessandra is a consummate pro. Did everything I wanted, worth your time. Be sure to ask for a private dance! GREAT kisser. - Tom S."* The last one made Joe ill, but he steeled himself and took some deep breaths. He began to force the nausea to turn to anger, and he quickly recovered. He made sure he wasn't missing any other little "gems" the website had to offer. Satisfied he missed nothing, he deleted his web history and shut down the browser.

Joe looked at his calendar but he had nothing of importance scheduled for the next few days, no court appearances or impending briefing deadlines. He needed time to work on this new project. He opened his email and scanned his inbox for the past month looking through the spam notices and found what he was looking for. The Chicago Bar Association was offering a day-long seminar on the new federal rules of evidence. These lectures were common occurrences, and Joe knew no one would think twice if he announced he was out for the day at a seminar. Each attorney was responsible for tracking their own continuing education credits, which meant no one would check if he actually went to a seminar. He spent a few minutes on Google Maps getting directions and committed them to memory. He checked his watch and closed down his computer.

Joe walked out as Ellen was settling in for the morning. She was a bit shocked to see Joe at the office so early, and he smiled and nodded.

"Morning Ellen, I am headed to that Bar Association seminar this morning, I may be back after 5:00 p.m."

"Oh, all right. Did you close down your computer?"

"Yep, all closed up in there," Joe said.

"That's fine. Because, you know, The Boss said we need to conserve energy so our computers should be shut down when we are away from the office."

"Yes, Ellen. I know. That's why I shut down my computer. To conserve energy. For the boss."

Ellen wasn't used to Joe talking to her this long, and agreeing with her to boot. She was at a loss for words, for the first time Joe can recall.

Joe spun on a heel and headed for the door. He made his way to the car and pulled out of the complex. He drove a few blocks to his bank's ATM and withdrew $300; it was a larger amount than usual and he would have to craft an excuse for the transaction on the drive in case Tina checked the bank statement online. He managed to get on the expressway heading to Milwaukee and decided that, if asked, he would explain that he was planning to take her out for an expensive dinner before she packed up and headed to the Dells for the summer camp.

He crossed into Wisconsin and began looking for his exit. Fifteen miles north of the border Joe spotted the off-ramp, pulled off, and headed east. He went about a mile, turned on a side street and into a drab strip mall parking lot. He saw the lighted sign announcing his destination: "Gabe's Spy Gear." Joe shut off the engine and climbed out of the car. He reran the script in his head, and headed inside.

Chapter 11

A bell rang as Joe walked in but the clerk declined to look up from his laptop, seemingly on purpose. Joe guessed customers here didn't really want a lot of attention. He saw two other middle-aged white men wandering the aisles, Joe was pretty certain their names were listed on a sex offender registry somewhere. Who else shops at a spy store, other than suspicious husbands and trench coat perverts? Joe put his head down in an effort to avoid all eye contact, which seemed to be the social norm for shopping at this particular establishment.

He found a section marked "Software" and began perusing the selection. He found several keystroke logging programs and selected a mid-priced option. He noted the cover of the package promised the buyer could "Monitor your kid's keystrokes to ensure predators stay away!" Joe sneered, suspecting no one who actually purchased this was a concerned parent checking on their kids. Joe's phone buzzed and he pulled it out of his pocket. He missed the call but the caller left a voicemail from an unrecognizable number. He pressed the voicemail button and was greeted by Dr. Phillips' voice telling him he was all clear on the panel of tests. Joe leaned against the display case and breathed an audible sigh of relief.

A voice behind him startled Joe. "Worried about something, buddy?"

Joe jumped and looked at a young kid staring back at him. He had dark-rimmed glasses, a satchel slung over his shoulder and some kind of skinny pants on. He couldn't have been more than 25 years old, and he looked like he hadn't shaved or even taken a shower in a while. It took Joe a minute to realize he wasn't a clerk.

"Oh, umm, I'm just, uh, looking here." Joe was flustered and wasn't sure what to do.

"This is a pretty good deal, if you want my opinion. It runs totally undetected, and you can catch everything they do. Worried about your kid or something?" The young customer let a smile creep across his face.

"Oh, yeah. You know, can't be too safe." Joe considered his next move, but ultimately decided asking this strange kid he will never see again for advice was safer than asking a clerk that might actually remember him. "Say, how do I get this on her laptop?"

"Oh, it's easy. You just slip the CD in the disk tray, follow the setup instructions, add your email and the program will record the keystrokes, webpages, passwords, everything, and email it all to your account. Takes like, less than five minutes." He was animated and spoke fast, Joe imagined the kid came to the store every day, hopped up on Redbull, hoping to find someone with which to share his opinions on everything in the store.

"Wow, sounds perfect. Wait, do I need to access her laptop? Because she has a password." Joe was worried it wouldn't be so easy.

"Well, if you don't know the password, you have to wait for your *daughter* to type in her password and then leave the laptop open. You can install it right away. But if you don't know the password, it's tough if you don't know what you're doing."

Joe considered this while his mind whirred. Tina always logged off, even if she stepped away for a minute. How could he get her away from her computer without giving her the chance to logout? He decided it wasn't an insurmountable task. Joe tucked the package under his arm and decided to press on. "You know, she's dating this older guy, I'd like to know where they go at night. I know they have these GPS things I can put on her car."

"Oh yeah, it's totally boss. These guys have everything." The kid gestured toward the clerk behind the counter, "Hey Wizzer! You gotta let me work here, man!" The clerk did not even bother to look up as Joe followed the kid around the store. They walked to another section and the kid talked rapidly as he tossed out acronyms the way Joe tossed out legal precedents. Joe did some arithmetic and finally interrupted his speech.

"I have about $200 left after the software here, what can I get?"

"Oh yeah, you definitely have some options." He selected a few and recommended one to Joe, promising it was small, almost undetectable, updated every 10 seconds in real-time and was accurate to within a few feet. Joe took the package and put it together with the software.

The kid seemed proud of himself and looked at Joe with a knowing smile. "So, how old is your *daughter*?" His emphasis on the word "daughter" disgusted Joe and he realized he was in a place he did not want to be.

"Thanks for the help." Joe turned from the young customer and made a bee line for the counter. The clerk barely looked up as Joe laid his money on the counter, grabbed his change and left without a receipt.

Chapter 12

Joe devised a plan on the way home and arrived just after one o'clock. He was surprised to see Tina's car in the garage and mentally shifted into something of a defensive posture. He exited the car, took a deep breath and walked in.

Tina greeted him with an inviting smile. The old Joe would have been enchanted by her warmth, but now he can't help but see her as a spider attracting a fly. "Hi, hon! Aw, are you still getting over the flu bug?"

Joe put his hand to his mouth and summoned a cough. "Yeah, worked half a day, which was enough. Why are you home so early?" Joe was watching her demeanor for any hint of deception.

"I couldn't get anything done at the office. I have to finalize each day's activities for the camp and some parents were calling me every five minutes. Drove me nuts."

Joe had to give her credit, she betrayed nothing to him. She went to give him a peck, but he backed away. "Still getting over this bug, you better not."

"Oh, sure. Can't afford to get sick now," she said. Joe sensed an opening and pounced.

"Yeah, I should stay on the sofa a few more nights. You know, just until it clears my system. Don't you have some kind of fundraiser tonight?"

"Oh, yeah. The fundraiser." Joe noticed her façade started to crack. "I need to get on my computer for a while, I don't have to start getting ready for a few hours." Tina made some chit chat while she poured herself a glass of water and headed upstairs.

Joe gave her a minute to get settled in her office and then went to work. He crossed into the kitchen and eased open the door to the garage.

He went to the car, removed the bag from underneath the passenger seat and pulled out the GPS device. It was heavy but compact. Fortunately, the instructions were relatively simple and it came with a small kit to attach to the target's car. He selected her model of car from the lengthy instructions and mentally went through the steps to attach it to the undercarriage of a Jetta. The instructions also described how to link a smartphone to the device through the company's host. He shook the batteries out of the box and inserted them in the device. Joe went through one last risk assessment, trying to determine how the device could be traced to him if it was inadvertently discovered. *The phone is untraceable and I paid cash for the device.* Deciding it was worth the risk, he stepped out of the car and eased the door closed. He placed his sport coat on the garage floor, laid face-up on it, slid under Tina's car and began to attach the GPS to the frame as described in the instructions. He threaded a thin metal brace through a flap on the device and located a section of the car's frame with an exposed metal gap. He held it against the frame and wrapped the ends around a small exposed hole in the frame, pinched the ends of the brace together and fastened the device to the frame with a screw and a wingnut. He gave it a few tugs and decided it was solid. He flipped the switch on the side to "active" and a green light began to glow. Joe shimmied out from the car, stood up and dusted off his coat. He slid back in his car and gently closed the door. He checked the doorway for Tina and began following the Byzantine instructions to link to the host server. After several minutes attempting to download the program to his smartphone, the screen lit up announcing the new application was loaded. Joe tapped the screen and within a minute, his neighborhood appeared on a map with a pulsating red dot over his house. Joe closed the app, smiled to himself and tucked the empty box in the bag and set it on the passenger seat.

Joe then opened the software package and read the instructions. This kid at the store was right, it was pretty idiot-proof, as long as he could get Tina to leave her computer open and give him about five minutes of privacy. He knew he needed an email account to which the data logs could be sent, so he used his smartphone to create a dummy Hotmail account and tucked the rest of the contents into the bag and stashed it back under his seat. He slipped the installation disc in his inner coat pocket and stepped out of the car. He gently closed the door and snuck back in the house. He listened for Tina calling to him, but heard nothing. He carefully slipped off his shoes and sat on the sofa. *Now comes the hard part*, he thought.

Joe picked up the phone and made a call. He spoke for a few minutes and hung up. He checked his watch and waited. He was beginning to enjoy himself for the first time in days. Another ten minutes passed and Joe removed his wallet, adjusted its contents as he passed the living room mantel and placed it strategically on the kitchen counter. He then made an excessive amount of noise as he climbed the stairs, coughing and sniffling as he approached her office. He glanced in and saw Tina looking at some mundane website and she greeted him lovingly.

"Feeling better?" she asked.

"Yeah, gonna take a shower." Joe stepped into the bedroom, carefully hung his sport coat in the closet and stripped naked. He wrapped a towel around himself and waited. And waited. Finally, the doorbell rang. Joe immediately turned on the shower and stepped into the doorway of Tina's office.

"Oh, shoot! Hon, I ordered some delivery from the gourmet sandwich place and the kid's here. Can you handle it?"

Tina seemed flustered. "Oh, sure. Umm, just let me do something first..." She frantically began typing and moving the mouse.

"Hon, *please*, I'm naked here." Tina anxiously got up and Joe called to her as she rushed past. "Thanks, hon!" As Tina scampered downstairs Joe slipped into her office and yelled down the hallway. "My wallet's in the kitchen!" He could hear Tina breathlessly open the door and speak to the delivery boy. Joe minimized Tina's browser and inserted the CD. It began to whir and he was immediately prompted to install the program. Joe frantically clicked the mouse while simultaneously listening for Tina. He entered his new email account and allowed the software to choose the appropriate settings, he recalled reading the instructions that it would default to some kind of stealth mode. He could hear her quickstep into the kitchen and return to the door. Some more whispered conversations with the delivery boy, and Tina walked to the bottom of the stairs.

"Joe? It's not enough! Do you have more cash?"

Don't you have some cash? Joe thought. He eased into the hallway and yelled back, as if from the bathroom. "There's another $20 in the tray on the mantel!" Joe ran back to the computer and watched the installation wizard estimate there was less than one minute remaining. He listened more and heard the front door close. He tiptoed to the hallway and yelled, "Can you just put out some plates and dish it up? I'll be down in…less than one minute!"

Joe listened as Tina hustled to the kitchen, frantically opened the cupboards and slammed some dishes on the counter. Joe checked the computer and nearly fainted when it appeared the computer crashed. But the screen flickered, the tray self-ejected the CD, and Joe snapped it up and reopened the browser. He slipped out of the office and placed the CD back in his sport coat.

Joe quickly jumped in the shower and spent a few minutes washing up. He dried off, threw on some sweatpants and headed down the hall. As he passed Tina's office, he noted that her browser was now closed and the screen demanded the user enter the appropriate password. Joe laughed and thought to himself, *you are sly, but so am I.* Joe casually walked downstairs and noted that Tina had their plates dished up for an early dinner.

"Sorry I didn't tell you hon. I thought you could have a snack before your fundraiser." Joe was feeling better now. This charade suited him quite well.

"Yeah, great. Thanks." Tina checked her watch, 2:30 p.m. "Well, I'm gonna take a sandwich upstairs and get some work done. I have a few more things to do before I have to get dressed." She corralled her plate, a cup of tea and a paper cup of fruit salad from the deli. Joe watched her walk upstairs and refused to move until he heard her office door close. He grabbed his sandwich and headed to the sofa. He opened his laptop and activated the browser. In the event Tina came down unexpectedly, he opened Google and typed in "Chicago Cubs All-Star candidates" and watched the screen populate the minimal results. Joe then glanced at the stairs and, hearing no movement, pulled out his new phone. He tapped the screen and accessed his new dummy Hotmail account. Joe recalled that the default prompt for the keylogger program emailed an activity report to him every hour. He opened his inbox and scanned the lone email, entitled

"Welcome to Keylogger." He closed the phone, slipped it into the pocket of his sweatpants and resigned himself to waiting an hour. He knew Tina was going to leave around 4:30 p.m., so he had some time. Joe closed his eyes for a minute and fell into a light sleep.

Chapter 13

Joe woke from his nap and checked his watch. 4:15 p.m., he'd been asleep for almost two hours. He listened for movement, Tina was rustling upstairs. He pulled out his new cellphone and checked his email. The inbox had one new message. He quickly opened the mail and a chat log emerged. Joe devoured its contents instantly.

Keylogger Report: June 18-2:45 p.m.

Outbox message

To: <Empty>

From: <Alessandra>

Cc: <Empty>

Bcc: <Client list>

Message body: Hey sexy! It's Ali. I have some free time tonight for Outcall, 5:00-7:00pm. Sorry, downtown only.

Report: June 18-3:15 p.m.

Inbox message

To: <Alessandra>

From: <JimAndStacy>

Cc: <Empty>

Bcc: <Empty>

Message Body: Hey Alessandra! No can do tonight, we have a parent teacher conference. Catch you next weekend, maybe?

Report: June 18-3:45 p.m.

Inbox message

To: <Alessandra>

From: <DrHouse>

Cc: <Empty>

Bcc: <Empty>

Message Body: Hey Ali! Good news, my surgery was postponed (patient got a fever). We can grab a room at the downtown Hyatt. Meet you in the bar at 5:00?

Report: June 18-3:47 p.m.

Outbox message

To: <DrHouse>

From: <Alessandra>

Cc: <Empty>

Bcc: <Empty>

Message body: Sounds great handsome, I'll wear something special. ;) See you there!

Joe heard Tina emerge from the bedroom and she walked down the hall. Joe closed the phone application as Tina descended the stairs. She wore a black cocktail dress, stockings and ballet flats. The hem fell to her knees and she wore a jacket over the dress to make the ensemble more sedate. Her hair was in a bun and she looked conservative at first glance. Joe's emotions betrayed him as he blurted out, "You look beautiful."

"Oh? Thank you. Well, I gotta go. I'll be back late, so you have to fend for yourself." She clutched her briefcase tightly in her hand and headed out the door. Joe waited tensely until he heard her car start and back out of the garage. He scrambled for his shoes and frantically tapped his new phone. He activated the GPS program and was transfixed by the pulsing red dot. He paused, realizing he knew exactly where she was going: the downtown Hyatt. He ran to the garage, started the car and peeled out of the driveway. Joe had to slow down to make sure he didn't overtake Tina, she was probably only a mile or two ahead. He took the most obvious route and opened the GPS tracker on his phone. She was indeed a mile ahead and was taking the same route. He sped up a little and settled in, periodically checking the phone. He saw her exit far ahead and accelerated toward the off-ramp. He spotted her taillights ahead and followed her to the hotel parking garage. He was careful to follow several hundred yards behind and arrived at the automatic gate, grabbed a ticket and pulled ahead. He spotted Tina another level up and he followed at a safe distance until she slammed on the brakes and grabbed a parking spot. Joe slowly backed up and searched for an empty space. Seeing none, he pulled into a handicapped spot and realized he could watch Tina behind him once he adjusted the rearview mirror.

Tina carefully stepped out of the car, walked to the back of the car and popped the trunk. She took off the jacket and placed it in the trunk. She slipped her ballet flats off and pulled a pair of spiked high heels from her briefcase and put them on. She took the rubber band out of her bun, bent over at the waist and shook her hair out. She stood up abruptly and snapped her hair back. Joe could barely recognize her anymore, she transformed before his eyes into someone he didn't know.

She casually grabbed a small black clutch from the briefcase, dropped the briefcase into the trunk, and paused before closing it. She slipped off her wedding ring and dropped it in the briefcase. She closed the trunk, pivoted and walked to the hotel elevator. She walked with purpose and her hips swayed in a way he never saw before. Joe waited until she was gone and decided to try to catch a glimpse of her bar meetup. Joe walked as quickly as he could down the parking ramp. He walked past the bank of elevators, descended two flights of stairs to the lobby and opened the large metal stairway door. Joe's pulse raced as he saw Tina merely ten feet away with her back turned to him, walking into the hotel bar. Joe turned back into the stairwell, closed the door behind him and began hyperventilating. He slowed his breathing and focused. He waited thirty seconds and checked his watch, 5:15 p.m. He again opened the door, slowly this time, and tried his best to look casual as he walked to the bar area. He found a rotund couple walking in and crouched behind them, peering over the female into the bar. He saw Tina approach an older man and throw her arms around his neck. He could hear her say, "Oh I missed you!" over the noise of the crowd. He was at least fifty, a bit overweight and had lost most of his hair. But he was well-dressed, wearing a suit and flashing a gold watch Joe could spot from across the room. Joe surmised he must have been waiting for some time because he motioned to a glass of white wine waiting for her on the bar. Joe wandered casually back to the stairwell, stepped back inside, and squatted down when the door closed behind him. He wiped the sweat from his forehead and, after a few minutes, gathered himself together and walked back to the bar entrance. Tina and her customer were already leaving the bar and were walking to the far end of the room to another bank of elevators. He had his arm around her waist as they walked and as they approached the elevators, he let his hand drift down to her rump. She giggled as she stepped into the elevator first. The client stood outside the elevator with a wide grin on his face when suddenly Tina's slender arm reached out from the elevator, grabbed his necktie, and yanked him into the elevator with her. Joe had seen quite enough. He returned to the stairwell and back to his car. Joe considered waiting in his car until she returned and confronting her in the parking garage for some kind of public humiliation, but he was too defeated for such a spectacle and decided to head home.

The time passed slowly and Joe paced around the house like a caged animal. He returned to the sofa at precisely 7:00 p.m. and was waiting there when Tina finally pulled into the garage close to 8:00 p.m. The blazer, bun and ballet flats were back in place, and her gait had returned to normal. The wedding ring once again prominently displayed on her hand.

"Hey babe. How'd the fundraiser go?" The tone of Joe's voice was dripping with sarcasm, which he was having trouble concealing.

"Oh, really great. I got a firm commitment from a physician and a few more leads. It was a pretty good evening, actually." Tina walked over to the sofa with her briefcase clutched tightly in her hand, gave Joe a kiss on the top of his head and headed to the stairs. "I'm gonna grab a quick shower and put on my pajamas. Back in a bit."

Glad you appreciated his firm commitment to you, he thought. Joe really admired her ability to lie to his face. She betrayed no hint of what happened over the previous two hours. She shifted gears from Tina to Alessandra and back to Tina without so much as a single mistake. If it wasn't for her carelessness leaving her phone out days earlier, he never would have known. He decided to sleep on the sofa again.

Chapter 14

The rest of the weekend was uneventful. Tina hung around the house while Joe constantly checked his Hotmail account for updates to her activity log but Tina managed to stay away from Alessandra. Joe assumed it was because he was around her too much, they were together in the house the entire time and perhaps Tina did not want to risk getting caught. The camp was exactly two weeks from Saturday, and he deduced Alessandra would be on hiatus until it was over. He decided the flu excuse wouldn't work anymore and Joe resumed sleeping in their bed. But he couldn't bring himself to initiate sex and Tina didn't express much interest either, which suited Joe fine. When Tina took her morning shower, Joe would do some reconnaissance through her dresser and closet as he selected her outfit for the day, but he found nothing out of the ordinary.

Monday came and their morning routine reappeared. Joe headed to the office and committed himself to checking his GPS and keylogger applications hourly. The GPS showed that Tina never strayed from her route: their home, to her office, and back. Joe found nothing new with the keylogger either, a few emails from prospective new clients but Alessandra refused to answer. Perhaps she had some kind of system to check them out before she met them, or else she had so many established clients she didn't take new ones. It wasn't until Wednesday night that Joe got a new lead.

Joe was in his usual cocoon on the sofa, Tina in her office. He checked his email through the smartphone and a new email log appeared.

Report: June 23-8:45 p.m.

Inbox message

To: <Alessandra>

From: \<GaryMax\>

Cc: \<Empty\>

Bcc: \<Empty\>

Message Body: Hey Ali! I know it's been a month, I was in New York for work a few times and you-know-who didn't go to her mother's house in Detroit at all. But she's gone this weekend, do you have any appointments Friday night?

Outbox message

To: \<GaryMax\>

From: \<Alessandra\>

Cc: \<Empty\>

Bcc: \<Empty\>

Message body: Well, I need to move a few things around, but I will make it work. Mmmm, can't wait! How much time would you like, lover?

Inbox message

To: \<Alessandra\>

From: \<GaryMax\>

Cc: \<Empty\>

Bcc: \<Empty\>

Message Body: Can I have you for the whole night? I want you to fall asleep in my arms again. I want to stroke your hair, I want to kiss you when we climax like last time. Pleaseeeeeee?

Outbox message

To: \<GaryMax\>

From: \<Alessandra\>

Cc: \<Empty\>

Bcc: \<Empty\>

Message body: Ugh, I can't say no to you sexy! Alright, let's meet at your place around 7:00 p.m.

Joe was reeling. *I had a few overnight work trips in the past, and a full week in St. Louis during that interstate bank fraud case last year. Is this when she did overnights? Tina does visit her mother in Peoria four or five times per year. Bingo.* The light went on in Joe's head. Just then Tina emerged and came down the steps. Tina tried to act casual but she clearly was distracted by something else. "Hey babe. I'm gonna make some tea." Joe eyed Tina suspiciously as she busied herself in the kitchen. "Listen, I think my mom's hip is bugging her again, so I'm going to visit her Friday night. Promise I'll be back early Saturday."

Joe was overcome with a sense of disgust at the sound of her voice as she spun her latest web of lies. Tina brought the art of deception to new heights.

"Aw, I was hoping we could grab a movie and dinner. Do you really have to?" Joe wanted to test her ability to call an audible at the line of scrimmage.

"That's so sweet. No, I really should be with her." Tina was a true master. Joe was impressed.

Joe stood, stretched his arms and said, "Well, I'm gonna hit the hay." Joe had taken to going to bed an hour before Tina so he could feign sleep when she turned in for the night and avoid having to make a romantic advance on someone he completely and thoroughly despised. A woman who had sex with God knows how many men. And women. Watching the doctor at the hotel bar paw at her like some drunken teenager, and then seeing Tina giggle as he did it, was the last straw. Joe didn't know what his next move was, so he decided to keep gathering information and hope a solution presented itself.

Chapter 15

Friday arrived and Joe went through his morning routine with Tina. He selected a drab outfit for Tina that was more appropriate for a nineteenth century schoolmarm: beige, floral print floor-length dress and a pair of mocha low-heeled pumps with a gold buckle across the top. But Tina dutifully donned the outfit without complaint. He watched her carefully, attempting to divine information about her evening's plans from some kind of subtle, nonverbal cue, hoping she would reveal something in the way she applied her makeup or styled her hair. But she betrayed nothing.

"So hon, are you coming home after work?" Joe asked innocently.

Tina continued adjusting her makeup without missing a beat. "No, I will probably head right from the office to Peoria. Need to get on the road and beat the traffic."

"Well, drive safe. Should I call you before bed?" Joe was having fun again.

Tina paused. "Um, you better let me call you. If mom knows you are calling, she'll want to talk your ear off. You know how she is."

"Aw, she is so sweet. I don't mind chatting with her for a bit." Joe was suppressing a smile at this point, but Tina wouldn't take the bait.

"How many sons-in-law would say that? You are something else, Joe." Joe noted that she changed the topic ever so slightly and never did say whether he should call or not. He decided not to push it, especially if he was going to be keeping an eye on her anyway.

Tina finished in the bathroom and headed downstairs. Joe finished combing his hair over the top of his head, walked to the bedroom and selected a crimson bow tie to go with black slacks and shoes and a dark gray jacket.

Joe walked down to the kitchen and watched Tina scramble to grab a muffin and fill her travel mug from the coffee pot. He leaned back on the counter and let a smile creep across his lips. *Run, little rabbit. Run, run, run.* She headed for the door and promised Joe she'd call him later tonight. *Huh, she didn't forget. Very smart.*

Joe arrived at the office precisely on time. He exited his car, looked to make sure no one was nearby, and subtly grabbed the bag he stashed under his seat. He walked calmly through the parking garage and slipped the bag containing the trash from the spy store into a garbage can and continued through into the elevator and went to the office. He walked through the reception area and rapped his knuckles on Ellen's desk as he passed by. Ellen looked up from her computer briefly.

"Good morning, Joe. Hey, are you finally feeling better? You look good." Ellen was pleased with her compliment.

Joe was beaming as he strode past her desk. "Ellen, I feel great. If a man has his health, he has everything. Right?"

Ellen looked at Joe as if he suddenly grew a second head. She wasn't used to seeing Joe so chipper in the morning. Or anytime, really.

"Well, I suppose so," she muttered.

Joe accomplished little that day. He checked his phone constantly, but the GPS showed Tina at her office and there were no new emails to or from Alessandra. He spent the afternoon shoving files around his desk while simultaneously glancing at his lap to check the phone. He was scanning the phone when he was startled by the sound of a throat clearing. Joe looked up and saw Jackie Dekker standing in his doorway. She had taken to wearing pants around the office, Joe must not have been the only one watching her hemline. Of course, that meant Ellen complained. There was probably some obscure dress code regulation regarding hemlines of statuesque former collegiate volleyball players. But the directive did no good whatsoever, Jackie looked as good in tight slacks and heels as anything else.

"Joe? I am working on the sentencing guidelines for that check fraud case, and I am getting a little stuck. Can I get you to double check my arithmetic?"

Joe brightened up and motioned her over. "You bet, let's take a look. It took me a couple years to get a handle on the sentencing guidelines, so don't expect to get it all at once."

In 1986, Len Bias was the University of Maryland basketball phenom entering the NBA draft. Coming two years after Michael Jordan was drafted by the Chicago Bulls, the two were poised to offer fans the next generation of a Magic Johnson – Larry Byrd style rivalry. On June 17, he was drafted number one overall by the Boston Celtics. Less than 48 hours later, he was dead from an overdose of powder cocaine (not crack cocaine, contrary to popular belief). Congressmen returning to their home districts for the summer were shocked to find Reaganomics and the Cold War threat took a backseat to Len Bias and a "get tough" attitude on crime. Always the type to run out in front of a parade after it already started, elected officials raced to the microphones proclaiming themselves tougher on crime than the next guy. As a result, the newly-created US Sentencing Commission went into overdrive and harsh mandatory minimums were quickly imposed for federal offenses. The centuries-old institution of judicial discretion in sentencing convicted criminals was now considered on par with gonorrhea. Judges were handed a lengthy sentencing matrix that resembled Egyptian hieroglyphs and practitioners across the country scrambled to make sense of it. New attorneys like Jackie would need a few years to truly understand how to apply the non-negotiable criteria to, for example, a first offense non-cooperating defendant versus a career criminal who confessed and ratted out his co-conspirators.

Joe swiveled in his chair and scooted around to sit closer to Jackie. He looked at the computations on Jackie's yellow legal pad and began making some notes, but immediately became distracted by her perfume. It was intoxicating. As Jackie leaned in to read Joe's writing, he leaned closer to smell her hair. Joe quickly made a game of it, writing small, illegible notes in the margin to force Jackie to lean in to read them so that he could lean across and smell her hair. She finally leaned back and Joe cleared his throat and handed her the pad of paper.

"Well, you got it pretty much right. But you didn't deviate down far enough for the defendant's cooperation with our office. Judge Matthews tends to give them more credit for that, so you should take that into account and give him a lower range. I would say 27-36 months is a good spread."

76

"Thanks, that really helps."

"So, how are you getting along here?" Joe couldn't peel his eyes off her. She was nearly perfect.

"Well, the attorneys have been great. But some of the staff can be a little, um, cold." Joe knew this meant Ellen. She was the *de facto* leader of the office staff. *All Hail Queen of the Airheads.*

"Well, if you mean Ellen, keep in mind that she's staff, you're the attorney. If you get into a tiff, The Boss will back you. Just remember, she knew more than you did when you first got here. She got to be the Mother Hen, and Ellen *loves* to play the Mother Hen. Now that you're becoming wiser than she is, she resents you for it. Happens to everybody. Besides, she's a total bitch anyway." The last sentence surprised Jackie, Joe surprised himself as well. Neither expected him to say something like that; Joe never used foul language around the office. Or anywhere else, for that matter. Jackie burst out laughing.

"Oh my God, you're so funny! Well, thanks for the help, I'd better get back." Jackie walked out of the office, Joe watched her leave and enjoyed the show. When she turned down the hallway, he pulled out his phone and checked the keylogger report. One new email arrived. Joe opened the Hotmail account, *Alessandra told GaryMax* she was leaving her office around 4:00 p.m. Joe checked his watch, it was 3:45 p.m.

He immediately began powering down his computer and scanned the hallway. People in the office tended to get scarce by 4:00 p.m. on Friday, Joe saw Ellen packing up and decided to wait her out. Fifteen minutes later Joe checked his phone, opened the GPS application and saw Tina on the move. He peered out and saw Ellen zipping up her purse and powering down her computer. Joe checked the GPS and saw the pulsing red dot moving faster now on the Skokie Highway heading south. He watched Ellen casually rise from her chair and shuffle some files on her desk, causing Joe to curse her under his breath, *Hurry up you cow!* Finally, Ellen shut her monitor off and walked to the door. He gave her another minute head start and then shut off his office light and raced to his car.

Chapter 16

Joe quickstepped through the parking garage again but had to slow his gait to avoid undue attention from the other workers heading out for the weekend. He climbed in his car and checked the GPS, Tina was heading south from Waukegan toward downtown, but was still somewhere north of the city. Joe slammed the car in gear and peeled out of the garage. He fought rush hour traffic and cursed out loud at the gridlock, another thing he never did. Joe decided that somehow the cursing worked, because he finally made it to the Kennedy Expressway and accelerated north. He checked the GPS and saw that she exited somewhere in Winnetka, a zip code that Joe could never afford. After enduring a harrowing 45 minutes of North Chicago traffic, Joe was exasperated. He exited off the Edens and pulled over to check the GPS, she was somewhere east, just a few miles away. Joe drove and tried to navigate at the same time, but it became increasingly difficult. He nearly rear-ended an Audi and chastised himself for not demonstrating more self-control. Joe simultaneously slowed down the car and his breathing and he suddenly realized he was completely surrounded by seven and eight figure homes. The more obscene properties were betrayed only by a driveway and a thick grove of trees. The mansions were set back too far to be seen by a passerby.

Winnetka is an upscale North Chicago suburb on the shores of Lake Michigan. But simply calling it "upscale" is akin to calling Heidi Klum "aesthetically pleasing." It is one of the wealthiest suburbs in America and is designed to let the unwashed masses of urban Chicago know that they don't belong on those occasions when a Toyota Corolla like Joe's inadvertently crosses the border. In striking contrast to downtown Chicago's glass and steel monstrosities, Winnetka stands out for its one story buildings and four story homes. The jet set of Chicago's financial district and franchise-tag athletes seek refuge in the genteel style and slow pace of life afforded its affluent residents. Mutual of Omaha's Wild Kingdom once described the North American Winnetka Housewife as a species that simply does not engage in manual labor and mates only when in heat. The male of the species mates occasionally with its spouse, often with its secretary. The courtship ritual between the two typically involves a credit check and a visit to the matrimony lawyer for a prenup. The lawns are perfectly manicured and the homeowner's association has more muscle than Stalin. Legend has it a penny-wise Winnetka housewife going through a divorce once attempted to hold an actual rummage sale in an effort to clear out their His-And-Hers wave runners and her lousy cheating husband's set of Pings. The HOA convened an emergency meeting and the offending housewife was never heard from again.

Joe checked the GPS on his phone and it appeared Tina's car stopped somewhere in the immediate area. Joe drove slowly past two gaudy concrete lions standing guard on either side of the mouth of a winding driveway leading to a red brick monstrosity. Joe peered out the passenger-side window at the black Mercedes in the driveway, parked next to two small children's bikes, complete with pink tassels hanging from the handlebars. Joe slammed on the brakes when he saw Tina's Jetta tucked behind the Mercedes, hidden next to the side entrance.

Joe drove around the subdivision and decided he was too conspicuous to drive in circles or park on the street. He drove several miles to the west and made a five-mile loop, passing the house several times. He decided to get a burger and give it some time. He found a McDonald's in Northbrook a few miles to the west and sat in his car with the GPS open. Tina's car never moved. He ate his burger and watched the sun go down. By 9:00 p.m. and with only a half a tank of gas left, Joe headed back to the subdivision. He drove slowly past Tina's client's house and spied her car still parked in the driveway. Joe parked across the street, deciding it was dark enough that he could escape notice. He sat back in his seat and checked the home's windows for any sign of movement. After an hour, a small light came on in a second story room in the center of the upper level; Joe surmised Tina was hiding out in the bathroom. Joe sat bolt upright, trying to make out any movement behind the drawn curtains. Suddenly, his phone rang. Joe pulled out his old phone and saw Tina's number light up the screen. He took a breath and answered.

"Hello? Tina?"

Tina was practically whispering. "Hey hon. Sorry I'm calling so late. How is your night going?"

Joe's wrath was building again and he had to control himself. "Fine, just sitting here. Wishing I could see you," Joe said, as he gazed at the lit powder room window.

"Aw, that's sweet." She sounded so genuine. Joe pictured her standing in front of the bathroom mirror wearing some kind of leather outfit that those women wear, reapplying her lipstick and whispering into the phone while her client lie in an oversized bed in the next room, popping another Viagra tablet to get ready for Act II, Scene I.

Joe clenched his jaw. "Can I say 'hi' to your mom?"

"Aw, no hon. She's asleep. I have to keep this short, I don't want her to wake up. It took her awhile to fall asleep. You know, her hip."

"Yeah, well, give mom a big, ol' wet kiss for me." Joe was slowly, but forcefully, punching the steering wheel.

"Ok, hon. Night. Love you."

Joe could only manage a weak, "Mm-hmm" in response. Tina hung up and Joe threw the phone on the floor. He looked up and saw the bathroom light switch off. Joe imagined what they did over the last four hours, what else they were going to do the rest of the night and into the morning. *Would they have sex in the morning? Tina and I did that a few times but she didn't seem to enjoy it. Would she cook him breakfast? Did she rush to his bed after she hung up? Was she resting in his arms? Kissing him? French kissing him?* He started to feel nauseous.

Joe sat in his car for hours, getting more upset with each passing minute. By 3:00 a.m., he was apoplectic and needed to do something. Anything. He finally eased out of the car and tried to casually walk to the mouth of the driveway, looking up and down the street for any signs of life. The lack of streetlights and glut of overgrown trees on every lot gave *GaryMax* and his neighbors total privacy. *Nothing to see here folks, just a pissed off husband wandering Winnetka at 3:00 a.m. looking to confront his whore of a wife.*

Joe hadn't really mapped out a plan, other than to break down the door and pummel *GaryMax* to a bloody pulp. He has not been in a fistfight since Mick Pearsall told him his Keds were "gay" in the fourth grade, so he would have to engage in some on-the-job training. He arrived at the mouth of the driveway and paused. *Okay, here we go.* Joe quietly walked up the drive and approached Tina's car. He froze when he saw movement at the side door. He ducked down behind the black Mercedes and peered around the corner. Tina stepped out and looked like a complete stranger. Illuminated by a dim light coming from the back of the house, he saw that she wore a black floor length cocktail gown, one Joe never saw before. Between the house and the office, Tina ditched the floral print dress and brown pumps. She wore the same spiked black heels from the hotel bar and sported a long black scarf draped around her neck. She had an expression on her face that Joe took for one of smugness. Joe wanted her to experience the same shame he had been feeling since he discovered her betrayal, and a public humiliation in this rich clown's driveway would surely suffice. Tina quietly closed the side door, reached above the door frame and fished out a key, locked the door and returned it above the door. *She knows where he keeps the door key.* She turned from the house and walked toward her car, Joe ducked back and waited for the chance to surprise her. The look on her cheating face was going to be priceless. She paused, and Joe peered out again. Tina was facing away from him now, leaning on the driver's side door of her Jetta. She carefully placed her back clutch purse on the roof, bent awkwardly to the side and lifted her dress up slightly. She wiggled her hips and pulled her panties down and stepped out of them. They were some kind of black lace thing that Joe never saw her wear in their home. She stuffed them into her clutch and snapped it shut. A switch in Joe's mind was thrown at the spectacle of it all. The rage of the last six hours, the last few weeks. It was too much for Joe.

He approached her from behind and grabbed her forcefully around the neck. Her sheer scarf served as a poor buffer from his grip. She dropped her keys and purse as Joe lifted her off the ground. She tried in vain to grab Joe's hands and kicked her legs feebly, but she made no other sounds. Joe's rage grew as his grip intensified. He screamed inside of his own mind: *Shut up, shut up, you filthy whore! You filthy, filthy whore!* He clenched

81

his teeth and squeezed his eyes shut. He began to feel a sharp burn in his arms and eased his grip and opened his eyes. He never felt Tina stop struggling, she was now limp like a ragdoll. Joe released his hold and she crumpled to the ground, her head hitting the pavement as she landed on her back. Joe collapsed next to her, and noticed for the first time he was breathless and his arms hurt. Joe realized he must have had Tina in his grip for a full minute. He stared at her lifeless body and tried to process what just happened. He saw blood ooze from under her head and her eyes were bulging out. Her keys and purse lay on the pavement and her scarf was crumpled around her throat. Joe laid his head on her chest to detect a heartbeat but was greeted with only his own heavy breathing.

Wha-what is happening? Joe shook her lifeless body a few times but gravity dictated the response. *I don't…I can't…* Joe's heart was pounding harder, he started to sway and the driveway appeared to tilt off its axis. He climbed on to all fours and concentrated on a single oil stain on the pavement. He closed his eyes and slowed his breathing. *Tina, oh God. No, no, no, no.* Joe looked at her face and momentarily considered mouth to mouth resuscitation, but blood and foam was now oozing from her mouth and he knew it would be a futile attempt. Somehow, he just knew. He rocked back and forth and finally rested his forehead on her chest, struggling to hold back his tears. He turned his head to the side and listened for her heart one last time. But again, nothing.

He looked across her body and noticed the flat edge of the GPS under Tina's car and thought about the series of events that led to that moment. *What have I done? Oh, God, I killed her. Oh, God.* Joe bolted upright and paused to listen but the house was silent and he heard nothing from the street. No barking dog, no sirens, nothing. As if on instinct, Joe scrambled around Tina's lifeless body, shimmied under her car and removed the GPS. He stood up and tucked it under his arm. He began walking quickly to his car, unable to turn around and look at his wife one last time. He started to cry as his pace turned to a full sprint to his car. He fumbled with his keys, finally opening the door. He started the car, wiped the tears from his eyes and accelerated away from the curb.

Chapter 17

Joe sobbed the entire drive, a million thoughts crashing into each other in his mind. *The IRS? You were afraid of the IRS? This is murder, genius. Life in prison kind of stuff. Law license? Try Supermax.* Joe tried to clear his head. He turned onto the freeway and headed home. *Need to think…need to think, what the hell do I do with the GPS?* Joe made it to his exit and turned off the highway. He pulled over at a turnout on the south end of Minear Lake, a small spit of water a mile east of his house. Joe stepped out of the car and looked around, Libertyville was sound asleep. Joe reared back and hurled the GPS as far as he could. The splash momentarily broke the silence. Joe got back in the car and sped home.

He pulled in to the garage, shut off the car and got out, cautiously stepping into the kitchen. He was half-expecting the police to be there waiting for him, but the house was silent and dark. He ran upstairs and threw on the light in the bathroom. Joe saw his reflection in the mirror, he was sweating profusely and barely recognized the face staring back. He turned on the faucet and splashed water on his face. *Got to think. The GPS is gone. The keylogger was still on her laptop. The laptop!* Joe sprinted down the hall to Tina's office. The laptop sat silently on the desk, Tina hadn't taken it with her.

Joe unplugged it and considered his options. He could try to un-install the keylogger, but the forensics guys were genuine sleuths, they'd find a trace of it somehow. Joe scooped it up and ran to the car. He hoped the neighbors wouldn't notice his car coming and going a few times in the middle of the night, but he never really talked to the neighbors and Joe banked on his anonymity again. Joe retraced his route back to Minear Lake but several cars were driving around the area this time and he did his best to nonchalantly drive in circles until he was alone. Joe returned to the south turnout and pulled over, slipped out of the car with the laptop and reared back, and then stopped. *Wait, will the laptop sink? The GPS was a solid metal 5-pound box, no doubt about that thing. But the laptop is made of a lot plastic and plastic floats, doesn't it?* Joe frantically searched his brain for the lobe that contained his freshman year physics course but all he could come up with was the dialogue from Monty Python and the Holy Grail: *What also floats in water? Bread…Apples….Very small rocks…Churches…a duck!* He had zero time to test the theory about the floating laptop so he returned to the car to think.

How the hell do I get rid of this? Simply throwing it in a dumpster is incredibly risky. I can't just smash it either, there had to be serial numbers on it in places I can't even begin to know. He drove around for an hour running different scenarios in his mind. None of them worked. Exhausted and unable to think straight, he surrendered to simplicity and pulled into a fast food restaurant and shut off the car. Looking around and seeing nothing, he slipped out of the car and approached a dumpster. He opened the lid and saw a number of large black garbage bags. He grabbed one, quickly untied the knot and shoved the laptop inside. He paused and dug the new phone out as well and slipped it in too, then retied the bag. Joe eased the lid shut and hustled back to the car. He sped away from the lot, drove home and pulled into the garage.

He stepped out of the car and cautiously walked inside. Still no cops waiting for him. He walked back upstairs to the bathroom and peeled off his clothes. He started to put them in the hamper, thought better of it and instead walked down to the basement and threw them in the washing machine. Standing there naked, Joe tossed in some detergent, shut the lid and started the cycle. He walked back upstairs and turned on the shower He stepped in and let the hot water rush over his head. After an eternity of scrubbing every inch of his body, Joe shut off the faucet, stepped out and toweled off. He put on some clean underwear, stood in the middle of the bedroom and stared at his bed. *Their* bed. He began to replay the night's events and got dizzy. He walked downstairs, rooted through the desk drawers in the living room and snatched the bottle of valium. Joe took two pills and settled on the sofa. He closed his eyes and tried to think. *GPS. Laptop.*

God, I murdered my wife. My life is over. He drifted off just before sunrise and fell into a deep sleep.

Joe woke with a start, the sun streamed through the windows and pierced his eyes. He heard a pounding in his head, he sat up and rubbed his eyes. The pounding got louder and Joe tried to focus. The pounding was audible now, and he heard a voice yelling, "Mr. Haise? Cook County Sheriff. Mr. Haise?"

Joe half-rolled off the sofa and stumbled to the door with the blanket wrapped around his waist. *The police? What the hell?* His arms cramped and he struggled to hold the blanket. He opened the front door in something resembling a stupor. A uniformed deputy and a man in a suit stood in his doorway, looking quite sober.

"Yeah?" The valium packed a hell of a wallop and Joe tried to shake its effects and concentrate.

"Mr. Haise, I'm Sergeant Tate with the Cook County Sheriff's Department, this is Sergeant Scott. Is Tina Haise your wife?"

It all came rushing back in an instant and Joe began to panic. *Tina, last night. Oh shit.* His breathing quickened and his face began to lose color. All he was able to manage was a weak, "Tina?"

"I'm sorry sir, but there's been some sort of incident. She was found dead this morning." The Sergeant blurted it out with little empathy, clearly he wasn't used to breaking this kind of news to the family members of murder victims.

"Wha...Tina?" Joe began to sway as the evening's events replayed in his head. The officers lurched forward and grabbed Joe. *Oh, God. I'm under arrest. Oh, Christ.*

Joe looked at the officers and tried to ask what charges he was facing. "Wha...what, um, what...?"

They ushered Joe to the sofa and sat him down. "Sir, we are still piecing together all the details. Where did you say she was going last night?"

Joe hadn't told them anything about last night, they were trying to trip him up. And the Valium wasn't helping either. Joe mumbled, "Her mother's. In Peoria." He tried to think of what attorney he should retain and decided to invoke his right to remain silent. The Deputy next to Joe still hadn't released the grip on his wrist, and Joe was unconsciously pull-

85

ing his arm away in anticipation of the handcuffs. "Excuse me, but I need to invo…I'd like to call my, um…" His tongue was thick and he couldn't form his words.

"Sir, she was found in Winnetka, not Peoria. Sergeant Scott here is from the Winnetka Police Department."

"Winnetka, not Peoria. Okay." Joe was confused, the conversation wasn't linear and he couldn't follow what they were saying.

"Yes, sir. And we have a suspect in custody," Sergeant Scott offered.

Joe looked up in a state of shock. "Suspect?"

"Yes, sir. A resident in Winnetka. She was found in his driveway next to her car. Does the name Gary Maxwell mean anything to you?"

Chapter 18

The officers escorted Joe upstairs while he threw on some clothes and they helped him into the back of their squad. Joe was doing his best to overcome the effects of the valium, but the officers appeared to be convinced they woke some poor schmo from a dead sleep, told him his wife was murdered and that they had to take him downtown to confirm the identity of the body. All things considered, Joe decided that he appeared to be acting as any husband would under the circumstances. He caught them constantly looking back at him in the rear of the squad; he sat expressionless with his mouth agape, staring out the window.

They arrived at the Cook County Administration Building and the Deputy helped Joe from the car. The officers guided him inside and he was ushered to an interview room. Sergeant Scott followed and offered Joe a seat. He was a heavyset man, bald with a closely shaved goatee. He had piercing eyes, and looked every bit a seasoned detective.

"Joe. Can I call you Joe? I'm Sergeant Buddy Scott from Winnetka PD and I'll be leading the investigation. I know you're a federal prosecutor so I'm sure you know how this works. I can't tell you much, just that she was found dead early this morning. Paperboy found her in this guy's driveway. So you say she was going to her mother's last night?"

Joe wasn't sure if he was being played. A good cop never reveals how much he knows. He was fighting the grogginess but he realized it helped him play the role of a husband in shock. "Yeah, Peoria. She was in Winnetka? Who is the guy again?"

"Gary Maxwell, some kind of big shot hedge fund manager. He lawyered up so we don't know much. Do you know if your wife had any, um, *friends* you didn't know about?"

Joe considered this carefully. "I never met the guy. Do you know exactly why she was there?"

"Based on how she was dressed, it appears they were…more than friends. I'm sorry."

"Oh." Buddy was eyeing Joe to gauge his reaction, it was obvious to Joe. Buddy didn't suggest there was anything more than a romantic relationship between Tina and Maxwell, at this stage of the investigation they appeared to be going with the theory that this was an affair gone wrong. The fact that Joe was a Federal prosecutor probably steered them in that direction, the idea that Tina was a high-priced escort was never considered. But something wasn't right, and Joe piped up immediately when he caught his mistake. "How did she die? Was she beaten or sexually assaulted or something?" Joe knew human nature dictated that every relative of a murder victim wants to know how their loved one died, but only guilty men never asked the question. They already knew.

"She was, ah, strangled. She suffered some kind of head injury as well. It does not appear that there was any kind of non-consensual relations between the, ah, victim and the suspect. That's all I can say." Sergeant Scott seemed to ease his posture a bit.

Joe put his head down and cried. He wasn't sure if he was crying for Tina, his reputation, or his current predicament. Regardless of the reason, he let it all out. Buddy patted Joe on his shoulder and offered him a tissue.

"Here Joe, drink some water." He handed Joe a Dixie cup of water and Joe gulped it down. He struggled to hold the cup, realizing his forearms were still cramping from the events of last night. He put the pain out of his mind. "Joe, I think you've had enough for today. So we'd like you to make a positive ID, and the Deputy outside can take you back home. We can talk more later. You okay to take a walk with me?"

Joe nodded and Buddy led him from the room, down the hallway and into an elevator. They rode silently down to the basement and the elevator doors opened. Joe immediately felt a rush of cold air and the acrid scent of mothballs filled his nose. *Formaldehyde. The morgue*, he thought. Buddy stepped off the elevator but Joe stayed behind, frozen. Buddy had to step back in and guide Joe by the elbow out of the elevator. Clearly, Buddy has seen this behavior before. Buddy led Joe down the hall to a small room with a window and steered Joe to stand in front of it. Joe's breathing became shallow as Buddy rapped on the glass and a curtain on the other side opened. Joe saw Tina, lying under a sheet peeled back to just under her chin. She looked pale and cold, her eyes were closed. He'd never seen her like that: no makeup, no color, no expression. Joe couldn't move or speak. He managed to open his mouth, but he could only muster a nod. Joe swallowed hard as Buddy rapped on the glass and the curtain closed.

Joe swayed a bit and Buddy steadied him. "You okay, pard?"

Joe nodded again. Buddy escorted him back to the elevator and eyed Joe closely in case he dropped. The doors opened to the lobby and Buddy took Joe out to a waiting Deputy and slipped his card in Joe's hand. "We'll talk later. Deputy here will get ya home safe."

Chapter 19

Joe stepped out of the squad and thanked the Deputy. He walked in the house, closed the door behind him and plopped on the sofa. One thought ran through his mind: *Am I going to get away with this?* He slipped back into lawyer mode and replayed the events of the last 24 hours. *Any connections to me? Any loose ends? Probably a million.* Joe stood up, scooted downstairs and popped the washing machine lid. His laundry was still damp. Joe added some more detergent and ran it again. He thought about the laptop and cellphone. Those contained his fingerprints, DNA, phone numbers, Tina's activities, everything. They were his loose ends, he couldn't control that mess now. Garbage all around Chicago was picked up every day, a dumpster five miles away from a murder scene was nothing special. No, it would be a million-to-one shot that anyone opens that particular bag and digs through it. Million-to-one. He wished the odds were better than that, he watched defendants go away for life based on a million-to-one shot, but he can't deal with that now. Out of his control.

Any witnesses? The burger guy from last night, but it was five miles away and six hours before the murder. The connection was just too tenuous to implicate him, even if the burger kid remembered him. He paid cash for everything and bought no gas. He decided another shower wouldn't be a bad idea. Joe hustled to the shower and jumped in. He soaped himself and began scrubbing his legs when he noticed a stream of pink foam circling the drain. *What the hell...blood.* Joe searched frantically and found a cut below his right knee. *From where? Tina's heels. She kicked me when I stood behind her and, um, you know.* Joe thought about DNA, but it was a small cut and the blood never would have gotten past his pants. *Did the detective see the cut when they greeted me at the door? I was wrapped in a sheet, maybe not.* He finished the shower and blotted the cut with toilet paper until the bleeding stopped. He flushed the wad, grabbed a towel and ran back down to the laundry room. The washer was still going and Joe stopped the cycle and checked his pants. A small dark spot the size of a penny was there on the pant leg, but no tear in the fabric. Joe grabbed a bottle of bleach, poured some in and added the towel wrapped around his waist for good measure. The bleach would ruin the clothes, but that was explainable: Joe was a typical heterosexual male, screwing up the laundry was par for the course.

Joe had to process this. *What should I do now? I should do whatever an innocent person would do in my position. An innocent person would start making notifications.* Joe grabbed his phone and began looking for the family address book. A few minutes of digging in the desk in the living room, and Joe discovered the small, spiral bound book. He flipped to Tina's mother and began pacing. He stared at his phone and considered what he should say. *Hi, Midge? It's Joe. Great, just great, thanks. Listen, remember how Tina used to be alive? Well, not so much anymore. But she used you as an alibi while she had monkey sex with a hedge fund manager for money, so that should be some small comfort.*

Joe decided not to give her any details, they would come later. He thought briefly, and began shallow panting. He dialed the number.

"Midge? It's Joe. Joe Haise. Oh God, it's Tina. She's dead...I don't *know*, damnit! She was attacked by some psycho, alright? I don't know, I don't know. Oh, God. I have to go." Joe hung up as Midge shrieked in his ear. He felt pangs of guilt, deceiving her wasn't easy. The guilt eased and Joe went down the mental list. *Work. Need to call The Boss.* He dialed and waited but was greeted by voicemail. Joe began panting again while the message ran and he waited for the beep. "Dave, it's Joe Haise. My wife... Tina...she's dead. Some guy went crazy and...I don't know. I won't be in next week. I have to plan things. I'm sorry." Joe hung up and the faintest of smiles appeared. He was beginning to enjoy himself. Joe thought about calling some of Tina's friends and he found a few numbers in their address book, but Joe had no idea which ones he should call. He decided to deal with that later.

Joe flipped open his laptop and checked the Trib's website. A small headline mentioned a body was found in Winnetka and that police were investigating. Then he saw the last sentence: *Hedge fund manager Gary Maxwell listed as a "person of interest." Charges may be forthcoming. More to follow.*

Joe smiled again. *Wait, Gary Maxwell. Where do I know that name from?* Joe searched his memory while he struggled to make the connection. *Gary Maxwell...he saw his name at the office. Somewhere on my desk. Or my computer? Did I prosecute him once?* Joe tapped his temple. *Think. GaryMax, the email. Gary Maxwell, the hedge fund manager. Gary Max...Gary M. The website...he was a reviewer!* Joe recalled the review: *Alessandra is awesome! Petite body, but a bundle of dynamite in bed! Worth every penny. – Gary M.* Joe was really beginning to have fun with this. He decided to keep this in his hip pocket for now. He lay down with the blanket and evaluated the loose ends. *How could this go sideways? What did I miss?*

Joe shut his eyes and went out for a few minutes when his phone buzzed. He looked, it was The Boss. He couldn't deal with him at that moment and let it go to voicemail. Joe shut the phone off and lay back down. *Damn phone. The phone. Tina's cellphones! Shit! Shit...shit...shit!* Joe sat bolt upright and began to do mental inventory. *Is there anything that could be tied to me? New phone: she called last night. Could they figure where I was when she called? Shit. I will have to feign some reason to be in the Winnetka area, could they triangulate the signal to the house or merely the zip code? My late night burger trip, maybe. Yes, Tina never lets me eat burgers so I made a late night sojourn because she was out of town. At her mother's. In Peoria.*

Old phone: Sent that single text from the disposable phone, otherwise I can honestly claim she told me she bought a new phone, so I am covered there. Shit. When they find Tina's phones, things get messy. Why didn't I grab them last night? Joe chastised himself for not thinking more clearly. He needed to focus. Get his arms around this thing. *Alright, I'll deal with the phones when the cop comes back. What was his name? Buddy?*

Chapter 20

Joe slept for a time and woke up. He turned on his phone, he had five missed calls. He threw it on the chair opened his laptop and refreshed the browser. The story was now second from the top on the Trib's site.

"Dateline…Winnetka, Illinois. Saturday, June 26. Gary Maxwell of Winnetka, a successful hedge fund manager and CEO of Blackpane Global, was placed under arrest this afternoon following a tragic discovery early this morning. He is expected to be formally charged with First Degree Murder later today. A Tribune delivery driver discovered Mr. Maxwell bent over what appeared to be a body in his driveway sometime after 3:00 am. Police arrived minutes later and found Mr. Maxwell in his home wearing only a bathrobe and speaking on the phone. He advised officers he was talking to his lawyer and would make no statement. The victim's name has not yet been released. Sources indicate the victim is a woman in her 30s who was visiting Mr. Maxwell. Gary Maxwell, known in finance circles for his ruthless but calculating nature, is married to Veronica Maxwell. The couple has twin six year-old girls."

The situation had some context now. Mrs. Veronica Maxwell had her life turned upside down, she would probably take her twin daughters and leave her no-good husband. Joe was struggling to decide if he had sympathy for Gary Maxwell, arrested for a murder he did not commit. No, he decidedly did *not*. Mr. Gary Maxwell of Fuck You, Illinois, defiled Joe's wife for money. French kissed her. "Dynamite in the sack," he said. *I hope you rot*, Joe thought.

Joe had a number of things he needed to do: arrange a funeral, publish the obituary, notify an estate planning lawyer. Life insurance, Joe was pretty sure they had a policy somewhere. Tina handled that kind of thing for them and a six-figure check would certainly help ease the grief of losing his wife so tragically. Joe smiled. He couldn't act too quickly, it would be suspicious. He decided to wait out the weekend and deal with that on Monday. *Tina's camp. Shit.* It was exactly seven days away. Joe decided to wait until Sunday to deal with it. He met Tina's part-time assistant a couple times, a cute grad student in Social Work. *Julie? Julia? Something with a J.* He'd wait until the whole city knew about the murder and then he'd track her down; he didn't need another person screeching in his ear over the phone just now.

Joe decided a grieving husband would gather liquor and mementos of their life together, so he rummaged in the desk until he uncovered their old wedding album. He tossed it on the occasional chair and draped a blanket over it so he wouldn't have to look at it. He walked into the kitchen and grabbed a half bottle of wine from the fridge and a glass. He walked to the sofa, plopped down and turned on the tv. Joe watched television so rarely he had to relearn the channel lineup. He found a "documentary" about aliens arriving in ancient Egypt and teaching the Egyptians how to build the Pyramids, and settled in. Joe took a couple of naps throughout the day and dreamt of Tina. He was standing in front of the small window in the morgue, Tina was on the slab and the sheet was pulled back, but he only saw the back of her head. She didn't have a face. He began to wake up when he heard a knock on the door.

Joe grabbed his pants and fished the album from under the blanket an opened it to a random page and placed it on the table. He concentrated on his expression, a combination of complete exhaustion and surrender. He opened the door, Buddy Scott greeted him.

"Joe, remember me? Buddy Scott, Winnetka PD."

Joe tried to sound defeated. "Sure, c'mon in Sergeant."

They walked in and Joe struggled to avoid any hint of unease. Buddy sat down on the chair, Joe on the sofa.

"You, ah, you doin' okay there, Joe?" Buddy gestured to the wine, wedding album, and bottle of valium. Joe forgot the valium was on the coffee table, but decided now it was a nice touch.

"Oh, yeah. It's been a little rough. I called Tina's mom, she's a mess. I can't really deal with her now, you know?"

Buddy tried to comfort Joe. "Listen, pard, there is no playbook here. You do whatever you need to do to get through this. You hear?"

Joe nodded thoughtfully. "Got anything else on this *animal?*"

"Well, we know they had some kind of relationship. Her car had been there for some time, engine was cold. She was dressed for a date. We seized the, um, linens from the house. Found her wedding ring, looks like she took it off and stashed it in her purse during her date with the guy."

Joe exhaled hard without trying to overdo it. "I don't know what to say."

Buddy reached over and patted Joe's knee. "No worries, Joe. You'll be alright. Now, we found her purse, keys, wallet, and she had a good wad of cash on her person. Looks like he gave her some walkin' around money. Listen, Joe. What kind of a cellphone did she have?"

Joe slowed his breathing and chose his words carefully. "She told me she lost hers a few weeks ago, so she bought a new one. I don't know where she got it, she handled all that stuff and paid the bill, so I don't know what to tell you." Joe paused, "Why are you asking?" Joe waited intensely for the response.

"Funniest thing Joe, she didn't have it on her. Looked everywhere. We got a warrant and I had a crew going over every inch of the suspect's house for twelve hours. Zilch."

This was an unexpected surprise and Joe had to think this through. *She had her "normal" phone; she called me from Maxwell's bathroom. And no way did she not have Alessandra's phone with her. Where the hell did they both go? She wouldn't have accidentally left both phones in the bedroom. Gary Maxwell. Holy shit, Gary grabbed both phones and did something before the cops arrived.*

"Listen, Joe, I hate to do this, but we need to establish a link between Tina and this fellow we found her with. So we're gonna need to go through her things here." Buddy fished some papers from his coat and handed them to Joe. "This is a warrant issued by a Cook County Judge, you know the routine."

Joe nodded and asked Buddy to be discreet if they found anything about "…that Gary fella." Buddy assured Joe he'd handle it just right.

Buddy walked to the door, opened it, and a stream of uniform and plainclothes officers walked in. Several headed upstairs immediately and the rest split in two groups and circled the main floor in opposite directions. They clearly had some kind of game plan before they ever stepped in the door.

Joe sat on the sofa and contemplated his situation. The clothes in the laundry were dry and Joe stacked them in several scattered storage bins as if they were ready for a trip to the Salvation Army. Tina wore a scarf around her neck that night, so no fingerprints. His shin was still bruised, but that could be easily explained. Phones and laptop were gone. He tried to remain calm and project the persona of a grieving widower.

A young, lanky officer in a blue jumpsuit walked over to Joe and reached across his body. Joe leaned back reflexively while the officer snatched Joe's cell phone off the coffee table. "Excuse me, sir." The technician popped out the SIM card and inserted it into a portable hard drive. It whirred for half a minute and the technician ejected the card and handed it back to Joe. "Any other phones here, sir?"

"Ah, no. No, that's it. That's the only one, right there." Joe thought he may have overdone it a bit and was glad that detective was upstairs.

The technician nodded and scooped up Joe's laptop. Joe breathed a sigh of relief that he had nothing incriminating on his laptop as the technician downloaded the contents and returned the computer to Joe.

A voice called from upstairs, "Joe? Can you come up here a sec?" Joe tried his best to casually ascend the staircase, however one would do that. He saw Buddy's bald head poking out from the office, and Joe entered. A uniformed officer was bagging CDs and flash drives that Tina had in the drawers, but the assembled gang seemed focused on the 18-inch by 18-inch empty spot on the top of her desk.

"Joe, looks like there was a computer here, probably a small laptop," Buddy said.

"Oh, yeah. Tina's laptop. She always took it with her. You know, for work."

Buddy looked at Joe a little suspiciously. "Yeah, we didn't find it on her person or in her car. Not at her workplace either." *They already swept her office.* "Any idea where that might be, Joe?"

Joe was uneasy, Buddy's tone and demeanor changed ever so slightly. Joe knew that Buddy suspected something. "Gosh, I can't tell you. I just know that she always took it with her."

Buddy looked at the lanky officer lurking behind Joe. "Stretch, you ghost his laptop and cell?" The technician nodded and Buddy gestured to the rest of the officers in the room and said, "Well, let's bag the rest here, boys." An officer ushered Joe back downstairs to the sofa. Joe sat down and turned on the tv so he could have a place to point his eyes while he thought.

The laptop. It's gone for sure, buried under a few thousand tons of landfill by now. But where do they think it went? Gary Maxwell grabbed it and hid it in his house? A cellphone, sure. Two, as a matter of fact. But the laptop? The laptop was too big and most people aren't that rational after committing murder. No, they don't think Maxwell dumped the laptop, but they probably don't have any idea where it went. I handed Buddy a loose end, wrapped up with a bow.

Buddy left Joe alone and, after an hour, they packed up and left. Buddy reminded Joe to call him, "...if he had anything he needed to talk about." Joe thought it was a consoling gesture, but he ruminated on Buddy's choice of words for the rest of the night. Even though Gary was charged with murder, Joe wasn't entirely in the clear just yet.

Chapter 21

The next few days were a blur. Buddy Scott left Joe alone and Joe managed to get through his voicemails on Monday. Most were from relatives, one from his old college roommate, and Dunham left a message telling Joe to take as much time as he needed. Not a peep from Ellen, she must have had some prior obligations, but he was certain she supported him in spirit. By Wednesday, Joe managed to obtain a referral for an estate lawyer named Al Baker, the partner of one of Joe's old law school classmates. Joe set up an appointment and arrived at Baker's Evanston office dressed in jeans, a t-shirt and a Cubs ball cap. Baker greeted Joe solemnly, he seemed to have some kind of a script for meeting widowed clients. Joe was a little lost, but Baker was patient and steady and told Joe there was no rush to do anything. "Just advise me of which funeral home you prefer and give me a short description of 'your Tina' and I can take care of the publishment. I'll also go ahead and contact the medical examiner and have her escorted to the funeral home." The word "escorted" made Joe flinch.

Joe thanked Al and decided it was time he put in an appearance in the office. He headed downtown, parked in the garage and took a deep breath as he walked in with his head down. Ellen did a double take as he walked through the door, she looked stunned and tried to offer Joe her version of condolences. "Joe, I didn't think you would…you know. Well, gosh, we all just adored Tina."

Joe nodded dutifully. "Just need to check a few things. Won't be long." Joe headed to his office over the sounds of murmuring colleagues. He could feel their eyes on his back as he closed his office door. Joe shuffled some files on his desk and checked his emails. He noted some files were moved, probably someone was instructed to check his pile and make sure he didn't miss a filing deadline. Federal jurisdiction is a heartless bitch, and a prosecutor's wife's brutal murder does not extend the deadlines. Especially if the prosecutor assigned to the case committed the aforementioned brutal murder.

Joe heard a gentle tapping on the glass door and saw Jackie Dekker gesturing to the empty chair in front of Joe's desk. Joe waived her in and she opened the door. She was dressed impeccably in tight black slacks and a sheer blouse with some kind of camisole underneath, her blonde hair now past her shoulders. She extended her hand but tears began streaming down her cheek before she could say anything.

"I'm so sorry, Joe. I don't know what to say." She carefully wiped her eyes and walked toward Joe, passing up the empty seat, choosing instead to lean her slender hip on a vacant corner of Joe's desk. "Dunham asked me to check your files and make sure we didn't miss anything."

Joe offered her a tissue. "Thank you for that Jackie. And thank you for checking my files. I came in to make sure I didn't blow any deadlines too. Glad you have my back." Jackie stood back up and smiled and Joe prepared himself for a consoling hug of such epic magnitude that poets would weep at the majesty of it all. Instead, Jackie offered a reassuring grip on Joe's upper arm and said she would be able to pick up any cases he couldn't deal with. She tried to smile and left, Joe decided the squeeze on the arm and the view of her walking away was a good consolation prize. He resolved at that moment to begin exercising.

Joe sat in front of his computer and began devouring every article about the murder. He decided if they watched his internet activity, this was perfectly normal behavior. A number of publications picked up the story, but revealed no real new information. No mention of prostitution, probably because she was found in a zip code where a few thousand dollars cash in your purse was what you needed to tip the guy that cuts the hair of the guy that mows your lawn. Joe opened his word processor and began writing Tina's obituary. He surprised himself by having difficulty describing Tina's passions or hobbies. Joe was experiencing obituary writer's block, if that was an actual thing one could suffer from. He finally settled on some vanilla language.

Haise, Christina (nee Mueller)

"On Saturday, June 26, Tina Haise, wife and daughter, passed away suddenly at the age of 34 years. Tina will be forever remembered by her husband Joseph and by her mother Margaret Mueller. Tina will also be forever remembered by her extended family and dear friends.

"Viewing will be held at Saturday, July 3, from 2:00-4:00 p.m., with brief memorial service at 4:00 p.m., at the Lewis and Street Funeral Home in Libertyville.

"Memorial donations in memory of Tina may be made to the Her Way Summer Camp, at any Chicago National Bank branch."

Joe thought it was a little cold, but he really couldn't recall anything that distinguished Tina to the outside world, other than her summer camp. He spoke with Tina's mom the day before, she sounded defeated and the conversation was brief. None of Tina's friends called, she wasn't really close to anyone besides Joe. He dialed the general number for Her Way, expecting a voicemail. A young woman's voice greeted him.

"Good afternoon, Her Way. This is Julie." Joe stuttered but managed to say his name.

"Oh. Oh! Mr. Haise? Oh, this is Julie, we met a few times? I am kind of taking care of things here. Are you, umm, coming or something?"

Joe recognized the sound of someone completely in over her head. He decided to offer some reassurance. "No, Julie. Just wanted you to know that I am turning over the reins of the camp this year. I know this is short notice but Tina always raved about you. I am going to give your information to an attorney named Al Baker. He will call you and give you access to the camp's bank account to make sure your salary and expenses are all covered. So now you can do whatever you have to do to get those girls on their way this weekend. You're in charge now, it's your camp."

"Oh, my! Oh, thank you Mr. Haise! I will not let you down. Or Tina. Both of you. Thank you so much!"

Joe mumbled a goodbye and hung up. He opened his email and typed a summary of his conversation with Julie. Joe then copied and pasted the obituary and sent it to Al Baker. He knew Al would follow up and close the loop. Al Baker was drooling over the contingency fee from the wrongful death suit against Gary Maxwell, so an estimate of the cost for his services was never discussed. Al just said they would handle it later, and

Joe's signature on the fee agreement was enough for Al to hit the ground running.

Joe closed up shop and headed toward the lobby, but Dave Dunham caught Joe in the hall and asked him for a private moment in his office. Joe cursed himself for not being more stealth and he followed Dave down the hall. They entered Dave's office and sat.

"Joe, gosh, hell of a thing. Look, I had Jacqueline check your office and I think you are covered, so don't think about work."

Dave, bless his heart, was a great supervisor, but a horrible empathizer. "Thanks, Dave. But a little work would be a good thing for me right now, so I may be back sooner rather than later."

"Fine, fine. Well then...hell of a thing, Joe. Just a hell of a thing." Dave and Joe stood and shared what was supposed to be something of a sincere handshake. It felt forced and Joe thanked Dave and practically sprinted out of his office.

Joe walked quickly down the hall and received a few dour nods from colleagues, but he didn't want to be the host of a pity party and he bolted for the exit.

Chapter 22

The wake and service was depressing for Joe. Not because of the topic *du jour*, but because almost no one came. Most of the visitors were Joe's work colleagues, including Jackie Dekker, who somehow managed to look stunning at a wake. Hell, even Ellen came. *She'll probably take two hours of comp time next week*, Joe thought. A few of Tina's friends that Joe recognized from the wedding came, and Midge was only able to handle about 15 minutes before a friend took her home. Otherwise, Joe stood by himself most of the time.

Joe was apprehensive when the funeral director wheeled Tina out in a silver casket; Joe insisted the funeral director ensure the lid remain closed. Joe stood next to the casket in what may be called the most awkward silence in the history of Libertyville. His palms were soaked and he began nervously shifting his weight. He bent over and inspected the undercarriage and then closely examined the flowers that Dunham sent over. He paced a bit until guests arrived, but couldn't bring himself to look directly at the casket. Instead, he busied himself with phantom duties and constantly checked the parking lot to keep an eye out for late arrivals.

Around 4:00 p.m., the remaining guests settled in for the memorial service. Joe simply thanked the dozen or so assembled guests for coming and pulled out a small scrap of paper from his pocket. He talked briefly about Tina, and not-so-briefly about himself and his monumental grief. He concluded by promising he would uphold his commitment to soldier on with his career in the US Attorney's office, explaining, "that's what Tina would want."

Joe thanked the funeral home staff and left the building exhausted. The drive home was surreal, Joe wasn't sure what he was supposed to do with himself from now on. He lumbered into the house, grabbed the last two valium in the bottle and popped them in his mouth, chased with half a bottle of red wine. He cursed Tina for making him do what he did. *Why couldn't she just be happy? She threw it all away and made me do something horrible.* Joe struggled mightily to convince himself that Tina was a selfish bitch and he passed out on the sofa.

He tended to the burial plot the following week. There was no additional ceremony beyond the wake, Joe had enough attention for one lifetime. He arranged for a modest headstone and drew Midge's ire when he failed to include some sentimental "Faithful Wife and Daughter" language. He simply could not bring himself to do it, Joe's sense of irony only went so far.

Joe began to recover something of a routine in the days that followed. He made it in to work a few minutes earlier every day, until he finally settled back to his normal schedule. He spent a weekend in late July putting Tina's things in boxes, but was disappointed to find no smoking guns. No additional evidence of her secret life. "Alessandra" was now just a blurred face on an internet site that leads to a missing phone that is God-knows-where and a dummy email account that will never be accessed. Whatever electronic evidence of her little hobby that existed was stored on a laptop buried at the bottom of a Chicago landfill. Whatever carnal pleasures she shared with Chicago's country-club set are never to be spoken of again. Most of her clients were silently praying that the petite hooker with the dishwater blonde hair would never reveal their indiscretions. And the ones who recognized her picture from the Trib were probably silently thanking Maxwell for making sure their little "whoopsies" would never be made public. No whips, garters or homemade sex tapes, Tina's entire life fit into a dozen bins containing department store clothing and a small framed picture of a ballerina bearing some indistinguishable signature. Joe placed them all in boxes, taped them shut and stacked them in the basement.

The investigation into Gary Maxwell continued, though a month passed with no word from Buddy. One article mentioned Gary's high-powered lawyers were angling for a plea deal, but it didn't sound good. His defense team did the next best thing and exercised Maxwell's right to a speedy trial, which means that the prosecution had 120 days from date of arrest to jury pick. Maxwell was probably hoping the prosecution couldn't piece the case together in the short amount of time allotted. Regardless, the trial was still a couple months off. There was no mention of the prostitution angle either, Joe deduced that Gary must have decided that the police could argue it gave him additional motive for murder so he was keeping it under wraps for the time being. Maxwell can claim he would never murder someone he genuinely loved and that someone else must have done it: Acquittal. Or he can claim that murdering his lover was a crime of passion after an argument about her leaving her husband for him: Second Degree Murder, 4-20 years. But if it came to light that the victim was a pro? Well Jesus H. Christ on a cracker, Gary the Hedge Fund Manager just gave the jury motive for First Degree Murder and a life sentence. "Jealous Lover Snaps, Kills Mistress," plays better in the press than "Ruthless Hedge Fund Titan Strangles Hooker." No, only Joe and Gary knew this little nugget, and neither one is talking.

Joe began to exercise, as he promised himself, converting Tina's office into a make-shift gym. He also did something he hasn't done in over a decade: he ditched the bowties and began wearing regular neckties. He stopped the charade of the comb-over and simply cut his hair close. He began walking a little straighter, the previous month took its toll and the stooped shoulders were beginning to be replaced by something resembling a strut. He was careful not to appear happy, so he would occasionally report a "bad day" to Ellen, knowing full well the whole office would know to avoid Joe that day before he even completed the sentence.

Joe began occasionally letting Ellen know that he was having a "good day" and even wrapped up a mortgage fraud case that had been gathering dust on his desk for months. Ellen, meanwhile, reverted to her same bubbly self and rarely engaged Joe in more than 30 seconds of conversation on any given day.

One morning Joe was grabbing a cup of coffee from the office kitchen when he saw Jackie looking a bit down. She brushed past him with a depressed "hi" and scrambled to her office. Joe sauntered back to his and checked his email.

> To: Office Staff
> From: Office Manager

104

Re: Personal Grooming Standards.

Dear Staff: Please remember to adhere to grooming standards as referenced in the federal employee handbook, strong perfumes are not allowed. Thank you.

Joe sat back. *Ellen. She was the Office Manager. Jackie was down because Ellen clipped her for wearing perfectly ravishing perfume and made sure the whole fucking office knew it.* Joe decided he had just about enough of Ellen, she needed to go. Traditionally, firing a federal employee for being a cruel bitch is like firing a Major League Baseball Manager for using foul language. He needed to come up with a plan. No detail left to chance. Joe had himself a project.

Chapter 23

Ellen was a creature of habit. She arrived at precisely 8:00 a.m., took a 30-minute lunch, two 15-minute breaks, and left at 5:00 p.m. every day, though she snuck out early on Fridays. She immediately opened her email and internet browser whenever she sat down at her desk. She reviewed the office Intranet page, her Church's website for choir practice information, and the website for Fox News. In order to deal with Ellen, Joe had to work within that framework. Federal employees don't get terminated for alcoholism or being occasionally late. Ellen needed to screw up at work more than once and more than a little bit. The problem was that she rarely did. She needed a little help.

Joe spent an afternoon at the office reviewing his files and found a briefing deadline in a low-level fraud case. The brief wouldn't make or break the case, but a missed deadline would cause some heartburn to The Boss. He hated missed deadlines and required the staff to explain, in writing, where the mistake was: a mistake in calendaring, leap year added a day that no one counted, etc. Joe's brief was due in two days, he got to work.

Most of the legal issues Joe dealt with on a daily basis were the same ten things over and over; Joe and the other prosecutors just recycled old briefs. It wasn't uncommon to submit a brief with little more than the defendant's name changed from one brief to another. Joe spent half an hour on the computer scanning his brief bank and calendar. He had a brief due in a couple of days on a defendant's motion to allow for pretrial conditional release. Joe spent a few minutes updating an old brief and hit the print button. He pulled the brief from the printer on his credenza and carefully turned to the signature page. Joe signed the brief and backdated the entry so it appeared he signed it three days earlier. Joe waited until

Ellen left for the day and the office had cleared out. Joe grabbed a bright pink post-it and wrote "Urgent" in big letters and stuck it to the brief. He walked out of the office, checked for activity, then approached Ellen's desk and slipped it near the bottom of the stack. Joe knew her rotation was five days, so she wouldn't see it until next week.

Joe planted that seed, he needed at least one more. He moved her chair from her desk and rooted through her trash. *Plastic bottle, she should have recycled. Big deal. Banana peel, could attract bugs. Maybe a health issue? Okay, if I report ants in the office, and then I tell people I saw them marching toward Ellen's desk…Christ, this is pointless.* Joe ran his fingers through his hair and shut his eyes momentarily. *I can't have my fingerprints on anything else, I have to find an unwitting accomplice.*

Enter Nate Maddux. Nate is a prosecutor in the Public Corruption unit, though he put in for a transfer to the Financial Crimes Section and was waiting on Dunham's approval. Nate is an imposing, dark-skinned African-American who was raised by his maternal grandmother. He played a little ball at Grambling, but tore up his knee his junior year and hit the books, making his way to law school and then the prosecutor's office five years ago. He was something of an anomaly in the office, not because he was the only African-American prosecutor they had, but because he was a (somewhat) closeted homosexual. Most of the staff didn't know about Nate's orientation and Nate's grandmother most certainly did not know. It was never talked about around the water cooler, for several reasons. First, Nate would probably rip the arms off anyone who judged his lifestyle choice and beat them to death with the bloody stumps. Second, and more importantly, US Attorney Dave Dunham was an unpaid consultant to the Lambda Legal network, a national organization that filed lawsuits on be-half of gays and lesbians who suffered discrimination.

This is good. Nate is perfect. So what the hell do I do with him? The gay thing, gotta use the gay thing somehow.

Few folks in the building knew that Ellen loved the Baby Jesus. She was devout Christian who thought there was too much foul language and S-E-X on network television. She wore a discreet crucifix around her neck and occasionally hummed Gospel songs. But if you weren't paying attention, and if you didn't know the melody to Bringing in the Sheaves, then you would have missed it. Over the years, Joe caught her giving Nate Maddux disapproving glances when he walked by, but her cues were always subtle. Joe tapped his temple over and over as he struggled. *How can I use this?* It was after 6:00 p.m. and Joe was getting hungry. He needed to re-focus. Joe surfed the web and found her church's website. He scanned the pages until he found one that declared all the positions of Ellen's chapter on homosexuality. Nate Maddux would be happy to know that Ellen and her flock all prayed for his lustful, gay-having soul and that he would be forgiven if he just promised to spend the rest of his life satisfying his urges by masturbating in a sock. There was a "Daily Alert" tab that kept the flock apprised of the increasing threat of the "queer agenda." Apparently, the flock had a source at Gay headquarters.

Joe scanned the rest of the website and saw something about a "Nationwide Call to Arms." A gay pride parade was being held the follow-ing week in Milwaukee and they needed counter-protesters and, of course, cash. Joe clicked the tab and a webpage burst forth that was practically screaming at the reader: bright rainbow flags flapped over a Bible while cartoon sirens flashed, with the banner headline "Gays = Satan!" Joe knew this was his in, and he decided to set the trap the next day. He deleted his browser history, powered down, and headed home.

The next day, Joe arrived at work early and waited patiently for El-len. She arrived at 8:00 a.m. like clockwork and settled in. Joe sidled up to her desk to make some chit chat.

"Hiya, Ellen! Need a cup 'o Joe?" Joe was grinning from ear to ear.

"Oh my, aren't you just a regular Red Skelton?" Joe had no idea who the hell that was. Ellen was a bit nicer to Joe since the funeral, but not enough that anyone would notice.

"Well, gotta keep busy, you know. Losing Tina was hard, but I found strength in some Scripture." Joe eyed Ellen cautiously, seeing if she bit.

Ellen's eyes lit up. "Really? Well, bless you Joe. You need to find yourself a good Christian girl this time." Joe couldn't believe how inappro-priate Ellen's comment was. *My God, she is Satan's sister-in-law.*

"Yeah, you're so right. Well, not gonna find one in Milwaukee this weekend. That's for sure." Joe baited the hook.

"Oh? What's in Milwaukee?" Ellen was curious now.

"That parade, they're all talking about it. The Archbishop was even on the radio this morning, I think." Joe casually looked down and tapped his wristwatch. "Well, back to the grind." Joe pivoted and walked back to his office. He walked in, and immediately turned around and peered through the glass. Ellen turned to her computer and, sure enough, found her Church's website. Ellen read slowly while Joe watched. She carefully hovered her mouse over the "Nationwide Call to Arms" tab and did nothing. *Do it, do it, do it,* Joe silently pleaded. She clicked the tab and her screen immediately opened the page. Between the colors and the flashing siren, Ellen instantly knew it was inappropriate for the office. She immediately began clicking her mouse and, after a few seconds, closed the page. But it didn't matter.

Joe spent the rest of the morning waiting for Ellen to take her approved 15-minute break. At 10:00 a.m., she gathered her purse and stood. Joe knew she never logged out of her computer during her break, only at the end of the day. Joe watched her leave for the lunchroom and sprinted to her desk. He sat in her chair and called up her internet browser. Joe spent a few seconds locating the "Call to Arms" page and quickly set it as her home page. He closed down her browser and jumped back in front of the counter. He checked his watch, she'd return in 12 minutes. Joe returned to his office and grabbed a manila folder and placed a memo on Search and Seizure inside. He returned to the lobby and set it on the top of Ellen's stack. He then waited exactly eleven minutes and casually walked down to Nate's office.

Nate was writing something on his computer when Joe interrupted. "Hey Nate, you know that Conflict of Interest case you have out of the South Side? I came across an old memo, thought you could use it. Did Ellen give it to you?"

Nate spun around from the computer with a quizzical look. "No, I didn't see anything. When was this?"

"Well, let's see if she has it around here someplace." Nate dutifully followed Joe out to Ellen's desk. As they turned the corner, Joe saw Ellen approaching the office main door. Joe snatched the file off of Ellen's pile just as Ellen walked in. She walked between them to her desk while Joe stalled.

"Yeah, so, I remembered this memo and everything and I thought it might help." Joe nonchalantly handed the folder to Nate who reached for it. Ellen sat down, turned to her computer and opened her email. Joe was clenching his teeth. *The internet…open your browser, damnit!*

Nate began to mutter a "thanks" and turned to head back to his office. Ellen maneuvered her mouse over the internet browser and double-clicked the icon. Joe clenched the folder, forcing Nate to pause in order to yank it out of Joe's hand. Joe immediately turned his head to Ellen's monitor and gasped. Nate naturally did the same, and he immediately donned the exact same expression of total shock that Ellen did. The three of them stared at the flashing page's contents for the longest moment in recorded history before Joe broke the silence.

"Oh, my. Um, Ellen?" Ellen scrambled to close the page, but the damage had been done. Ellen turned to Nate Maddux and apologized.

"I'm sorry, I don't know what happened." Nate went from zero to ten on the pissed meter and stormed back to his office. Joe gave a disappointed look to Ellen as he walked back to his office while Ellen tried to figure how to change her homepage back to the standard DOJ intranet homepage. Ellen breathlessly entered Joe's office a few minutes later.

"Joe, I don't know what happened. You see, I was looking for some church news earlier and I must have accidentally reset the…"

Joe cut her off with a wave of his hand. "I understand, Ellen. These things happen."

"Do you think I am in trouble?" She was genuinely terrified. When someone who never gets in trouble actually screws up, it can be nerve-wracking.

"Maybe it would be a good idea to circulate the EEO policy on a harassment-free workplace. I bet Nate would appreciate that." Joe was trying not to smile. Nate would never report Ellen's mistake, so Joe would have to get Ellen to do it for him.

"Oh, do you think so? Because, I can certainly do that." She was beginning to calm down.

"I think that's a fine idea." Joe nodded thoughtfully and Ellen made a bee-line back to her desk. Five minutes later, with no explanation, the entire office got an email reminding them of appropriate and respectful behavior towards coworkers in the office, regardless of their "choice of lifestyle." Joe knew Dunham would see this from Ellen, with no context, and wonder what the hell prompted it. Joe would be completely out of the loop for that mess. Sure enough, a few minutes later, Ellen's phone rang. She spoke only a few words, turned white as a sheet, and walked to The Boss' office.

By Wednesday the following week, Joe received an electronic notice from the court regarding his missed deadline. Joe knew Ellen got the same email and he waited. A few minutes later, Ellen ran into Joe's office with his brief in hand and was practically in tears.

"Joe, I just saw this! I don't know how I missed it!" She was frantic.

"Oh, God. Ellen, is that the bail modification brief in the Hernandez case? Oh, no! You missed the deadline! Did the court order him released? Please, not him. Anyone but him." Joe conveyed a sense of alarm that was totally unwarranted. He knew the court sent those electronic notices out automatically and this kind of missed deadline was wholly irrelevant. No federal judge would release a defendant from pretrial confinement because the Assistant US Attorney blew a briefing deadline on a bail motion.

"I don't know! I don't know!" she bellowed. Joe calmed her down.

"Don't worry, Ellen. Just get it filed today and I'll call the clerk and then go smooth things over with The Boss." She seemed relieved and Joe strutted down the hall.

He entered Dunham's large office and closed the door behind him. They talked for half an hour while Joe did his best to explain that Ellen was probably better suited for the Civil Division on the floor below, where deadlines were far more flexible and she and Nate Maddux could avoid each other. After the website snafu and the blown deadline, the US Attorney for the Northern District of Illinois needed little convincing and ordered the transfer. Joe volunteered to break the news to her and walked out, heading straight to Ellen's desk. He motioned her to follow him to his office. Joe closed the door behind them and told her he had "great news."

"Ellen, the boss contemplated some kind of formal reprimand, but I convinced him to allow you to simply move over to the Civil Division."

"Oh Lord! Bless you Joe! You are a Christian advocate!" She hugged Joe and returned to her desk. She sat in her chair looking relieved.

Her phone rang a minute later; in what must be some kind of land-speed record, HR was already contacting her to coordinate the move. Joe reclined in his chair and smiled.

Chapter 24

Joe waited until the end of the day to gloat, and sauntered down to Jackie Dekker's office. She was still fetching, but the long, pleated skirt and flats certainly took the edge off.

"Knock knock. Did you hear? Ellen is moving over to Civil. Suppose we'll have a new office manager soon." Joe tried to suppress his excitement.

Jackie couldn't contain a smile. "Really? Wow, what happened?" Joe said he didn't know all the details, but he was glad they could all "go back to the way things used to be," deciding Jackie could fill in that blank herself.

He strutted back to his office and was greeted by a ringing phone and scooped it up. "Joe Haise."

"Joe? It's Buddy Scott. Listen, you know the trial in your wife's case is approaching and I'd like to chat with you about some loose ends."

The phrase "loose ends" made Joe instantly sweat. Joe tried to sound confident. "Um, sure, no problem. When can you come by?"

"Well, I'd rather you come to my office," Buddy said. Joe was now in something approaching a panic. A homicide detective only interviewed you in their office when they wanted you outside of your comfort zone. In other words, when you were a "suspect." Or a "person of interest." Either way, you were pretty screwed.

"Sure, give me an hour." Joe hung up and tried to compose himself. The trial was less than a month away, but there was a better than 75% chance the trial would be postponed. There is always a prosecution witness that can't be found or a chemist's report that isn't complete. Despite the fact that Maxwell filed a speedy trial motion, the defense usually doesn't object to a delay so long as they think there is an edge to be gained by keeping the prosecution off-balance. Truly, they are hoping all the prosecutor's relevant witnesses will come down with the plague and die if they simply wait long enough.

Joe calmly left his office and explained to Ellen's backup from the office pool that he had an appointment and likely would not return. Saying the words made Joe ill; what if he never returned? What if Buddy Scott arrests him this afternoon when he shows up? No, if that was the case, Buddy wouldn't have called and asked him to come in. He spent the drive over to the station trying to control his blood pressure. He couldn't quite determine where Maxwell's house was in relation to the station, but circumnavigating the Village of Winnetka for the first time since the night of the murder was close enough for Joe's comfort. He pulled into the lot and parked, took a deep breath, and climbed out of the car.

The Winnetka Police Department is housed in a one story red brick building with white trim. It sports landscaping befitting a hamlet of such resources, the station's manicured front lawn is rivaled only by the 16th green at Augusta National. The adjacent fire department is equally impressive, and Joe deduced the locals who paid for all of it expected their every need to be met upon request. It was located less than a half mile from the shores of Lake Michigan, prime real estate afforded Buddy Scott and his pals.

Joe walked through the door and did his best to appear calm as he asked the desk Sergeant for Buddy Scott. The Sergeant picked up the phone and said simply, "He's here." Joe stood for a solid minute, decided that made him look guilty for some reason, and sat down. Another two minutes passed, and Joe was getting nervous. Something is wrong, Buddy is making him stew. Joe decided to play along and he sat motionless trying to look forlorn. It must have worked because Buddy came right out to greet him. Buddy gave Joe a stern look and shook his hand.

"Joe. Let's go to my office." Joe followed Buddy and he felt many eyes on him as he passed through the half-dozen or so officers typing at their desks. Buddy opened the door to an interview room and ushered Joe to a seat. Joe had seen enough interview tapes from the FBI guys to know he was probably on camera. He wasn't going to give Buddy the satisfaction of acting like a suspect, so he played dumb.

"Joe, how are you holding up?" Buddy's voice displayed no real concern.

"Buddy, I am day-to-day. You know how it is." Joe tried to adopt a hang-dog look. He wasn't sure it was working.

"Sure, sure. Listen, Joe, the trial is coming up, got a status hearing tomorrow as a matter of fact. But it looks like it's gonna go in four weeks, so we need to clear up a few things."

Joe knew the phrase "clear up a few things" really means "you are a lying son of a bitch and we have you cold" in cop-speak. Joe looked at Buddy quizzically. "I don't understand."

"Well Joe, it's like this. We know Maxwell and Tina crossed paths about two years ago, there was some kind of big fundraiser they both attended at the Field Museum with about 1,000 other folks, although we can't prove they ever actually talked. But we can put them in the same room together, so we assume that's when the affair started. We sat down with Gary Maxwell's lawyer, and he's claiming he didn't do it, he really cared for her, that he just found her lying there in his driveway after they, ah, spent some time together, yadda, yadda."

"Is that his excuse? He just found her? That's some kind of a joke." Joe tried to act indignant.

"Yeah, it gets better. He says someone else musta killed her, someone who was watching her or happened on her at that moment. The paperboy that found her, maybe. Heck, Joe, he even suggested *you* might have done it."

Joe, as if on cue, exploded. "What?! He said what?! That sonofabitch killed my wife and now he…he…" Joe acted as if he was too upset to finish. Buddy leapt up and put his hand on Joe's shoulder.

"Now, now. You and I know he's blowing smoke. His lawyer needs to earn that six-figure fee and all. But, see, here's the thing, Joe. We never did find her laptop or her cell phone. The phone was prepaid, like yours, and based on the number you gave us, we can only establish that she called you a few hours before she died, probably from his house. And we can establish that you were within five miles of his house based on the last ping from a north shore cell tower. But I tell ya, Joe. That laptop and cell phone are real head-scratchers. Now Maxwell is trying to hang this around your

115

neck. And if you knew about the nature of their relationship, well, shit Joe, you got motive. See where I'm going?"

Joe didn't see exactly where Buddy was going, so he kept up the charade. "God, he is pure evil. He violates the…the…*sacred* bonds of marriage, murders my…my…and…and…he has the *temerity* to blame me for it? Or even that poor paperboy, for God's sake. So he's claiming he didn't do it?"

"Sounds like it. So we need to make sure he can't pin this on you. What can you remember about that night? Where did you go?"

Joe's tie was getting tighter, he had to hold it together. Buddy's excuse that he needed Joe's help to make sure Maxwell couldn't pin it on him was complete bullshit. "Well, I usually grab a burger, because Tina won't let me eat fast food when she's home. So that's my routine when she's out of town on business or visiting her mom."

"You recall which burger joint, and maybe what time?"

"Gosh, Buddy, I really don't. Could have been on my way home, but maybe I went home first and then went out later and grabbed some dinner. Yeah, I think Tina called later when I was getting a burger." Joe was sweating through his shirt, his sport coat was next.

Buddy nodded. "Yeah, see, we know you were somewhere south of Libertyville around the time she called you based on the cell tower pings, but we can't get any closer than that without a better signal than what we have. So we need to nail that down, Joe." Buddy calling Joe by name was beginning to sound scripted, this was getting bad. Buddy scribbled some notes in the file about Joe's horseshit alibi and furrowed his brow.

"Another thing, Joe. We didn't get any prints. See, the killer had his hands on the scarf around her neck. Oh, hey, can I take a real quick look at your hands?" Joe hadn't expected this, Buddy was clever to slip in the request and make it sound as innocent as possible, giving Joe no time to object. Joe offered up his hands, which shook despite his best efforts to keep them steady. Buddy pulled out a small ruler and measured the distance between Joe's thumb and index finger. Buddy asked Joe to put his hands on the desk and laid the ruler next to Joe's fingers while he took out a digital camera that was connected by a cord to a desktop computer next to Buddy. "Steady there, Joe." He snapped some pictures before Joe could ask any questions.

A uniformed Sergeant knocked and entered at that very moment and handed Buddy a file that he never looked at. The Sergeant tried to casually hover over Buddy's shoulder while Buddy concentrated on the digital photo that displayed on the monitor. Buddy turned his head and looked at the Sergeant and they nodded soberly to each other. Buddy mumbled under his breath, "Same."

Joe tried to glean something from Buddy's behavior, so he piped up, as if the comment was meant for him. "What's that?"

Buddy looked distracted as he scribbled in his file. "Oh, it's just that Maxwell's hands are the same size as yours. Doesn't really add much to the investigation. Just a…happy coincidence, as we call it."

Joe was ready to sprint for the door. Cops don't believe in coincidences, Buddy was being sarcastic. The fact that Joe's hands are the same size as the wound on Tina's neck is bad. He hadn't considered that in his "loose ends" thought process. But it also means Maxwell is the perfect suspect, the evidence fits him as well. "Happy coincidence" swings both ways here. Joe tried to shift gears. "So, Buddy, is this really going to go to trial?"

Buddy closed his folder and leaned back in his chair. "Well, the prosecutor met with Maxwell's lawyer yesterday. From what I heard, they talked about a plea to Second Degree Murder and a recommendation of 10-12 years. He'd be out in six or seven. Not sure who made the offer, but one side or the other torpedoed that deal. So we're off to the races."

Joe decided he had enough of Buddy for now and attempted to make small talk until he could extricate himself entirely from the conversation. Buddy tried to talk to Joe about baseball, but Buddy was born and raised on the hardscrabble streets of Chicago's south side, which made him a Sox fan by birthright, so the conversation went nowhere. Joe was still unsure if he was being played, so he nonchalantly checked his watch and Buddy, taking the hint, finally stood and thanked Joe for his time. Joe tried to walk casually out of the station. He climbed into his car and let out a long exhale as he headed home.

On the drive he considered his options. He could sit back and let the case develop organically, but Maxwell was obviously building a TOD-DI defense, That Other Dude Did It. Joe was That Other Dude. But if

Maxwell took a Second Degree Murder offer, Joe would be in the clear; no uncertainty of a jury verdict, no cross-exam under oath with a perjury charge or, God forbid, a murder charge at risk. If Maxwell's lawyer waits until Joe's cross examination to drop the prostitution bomb, Joe's career is over, Maxwell might get acquitted, and Joe would become a *bona fide* suspect, at least in the eyes of the public, if not the State's Attorney's office. Joe didn't like Gary Maxwell pushing him around, he decided to push Gary back.

Chapter 25

Joe went home convinced that Buddy knew more than he let on, so Joe decided to regroup. He ran to the basement and pulled out a box marked "Tina's Stuff." Joe rummaged through the box until he retrieved an old photo album. He went upstairs to the living room and set the album on the coffee table and began rooting through the desk. He emerged with an old "Edwards in '08" campaign button and a pen knife. Joe was an Edwards supporter who was disappointed in his primary loss and disillusioned in his personal failings. He began leafing through the picture album, looking at photographs of Tina as a girl. She was always in a leotard or a tutu, smiling with her light blonde hair in a ponytail. He flipped past a few pictures from some early birthday parties. Tina was always next to the cake with her mom, just the two of them in their modest kitchen. He glanced at a few more of her in the background of some high school dance production, and then one of her graduation from college. Joe found some of their wedding pictures, and pulled out one of a close-up of Tina. He went to work.

The next morning Cook County Judge Terrance Holmes was plowing through his Status docket, trying to decide if he is really going to block off a week of his calendar for a jury trial, or if the defendants are going to come to their senses and plead out. Holmes was known for his belief that jury trials were nothing more than a scripted circus and he developed a reputation for giving substantial consideration to defendants that saved the taxpayers of Cook County (not to mention His Honor) the time and expense of a trial. Holmes spent twelve years as a public defender before being appointed to a vacancy created when his predecessor, the Honorable Seamus Cullen, was caught in chambers *in flagrante delicto* with a defendant charged with prostitution. Seamus blamed the momentary lapse in judgment on his drinking problem, the stress of the job and even "that damn strumpet," all to no avail. A number of Cook County Courthouse rats began jockeying for the seat even before Seamus zipped up, but Holmes' experience as a public defender, coupled with his father's generous contributions to Democratic causes over the last ten years, clinched the appointment. The Chicago Democratic machine ran through the Courthouse as well as the Statehouse. This day a few cases pled out and a few more were dismissed when the prosecutor advised the court that the complaining witness refused to cooperate. The morning wore on and Judge Holmes noted a few reporters began to appear and settle in the back of the courtroom. He casually leafed through the court docket and discovered the case that drew so much attention. He went rapid-fire through a few more cases until his clerk called the case everyone was waiting for. "Calling State of Illinois versus Gary Maxwell!"

The prosecutor grabbed the appropriate file from a box under the table. The defense attorney arose from the jury box, shuffled past a number of other defense attorneys looking jealous of their colleague who was about to get some good ink, and made his way to counsel table. A door off to the side of the courtroom opened and a large bailiff and a distinguished-looking man in his 50s emerged in a jumpsuit and shackles and frog-walked to the defense table. There was a palpable sense of excitement as the reporters and onlookers strained for a better view. All the parties finally settled in as Judge Holmes began to speak.

"I see that-" He stopped at the sound of movement and looked up, and suddenly the entire courtroom turned to see the commotion in the back of the room.

Joe Haise flung the doors open and entered the courtroom with a flourish. He strutted to the front row and took a seat immediately behind the prosecutor. He had a small Bible in one hand, and a button on his lapel with a small pink ribbon and a large, smiling picture of Tina at the center. Joe made sure everyone saw him cast a stern, disapproving look at Gary Maxwell. The handful of reporters, all of whom were quite disinterested before Joe's entrance, now leaned forward and began scribbling furiously. Judge Holmes adjusted his robe and cleared his throat over the murmurs now rippling through the gallery.

"Well, now. I see here we are on for Status today. And where are we Mr. Prosecutor?"

The prosecutor could not have been more than 30, and was probably simply covering the Felony calendar that day. He cleared his throat and stood, his voice briefly cracking as he spoke. "The State is ready to proceed to trial, your Honor."

The defense attorney was Jack Taggart, a well-dressed veteran with thin, red hair. He saw the media interest and savored the additional attention. He also stood and addressed the court, more clearly than his counterpart. "Your Honor, my client and I are also prepared for trial." The judge nodded and the defense counsel retook his seat. Both attorneys began leafing through their calendars, Gary Maxwell craned his neck and never took his eyes off Joe.

"Well, I see a speedy trial motion was made previously. So we will commence trial 30 days hence, beginning Monday August 4. We are adjourned." Holmes would have banged his gavel to add some theater to the moment, but after a brief search he realized that, like most judges, his only gavel was glued to a plaque in his office. The bailiffs quickly ushered Gary out of the courtroom, but he strained to maintain eye contact with Joe as he went. Joe stood and reached over the bar, shaking the puzzled prosecutor's hand. He walked out of the courtroom, trailed by several reporters flipping pages in their notebooks and fishing tape recorders out of their pockets.

"Mr. Haise? Do you have anything to say to Gary Maxwell? Are you confident in a Guilty verdict?"

Joe stopped and let them gather their notepads. "I am looking forward to the day of judgment, and I am sure the jury will offer no quarter to that evil man. For God will bring every deed into judgment, including every hidden thing, whether it is good or evil. Ecclesiastes, Chapter 12, Verse 14." Joe pulled the quote from a Bible website the night before, although he didn't know exactly what it meant. Joe looked on as the reporters quickly took down the quotes. He thanked them and headed for the nearest exit. The gaggle of reporters let Joe escape while they ran back to get a competing quote from Jack Taggart.

Joe dashed home and opened his browser. The Trib already had a line about the "tense" hearing in State v. Maxwell, and that the parties were gearing up for trial. Joe enjoyed turning up the heat on Maxwell, but he needed to do more.

Joe called the Victim/Witness coordinator for the Cook County State's Attorney's office and told the receptionist he wanted to speak to the prosecutor who would try the case. Joe left his information with the receptionist and was promised a return call. The prosecutor must have been fielding media calls all morning because Joe's phone rang a few minutes later.

"Mr. Haise? This is Bill McDonald, I'm calling from the Cook County State Attorney's Office and I'll be trying the Maxwell case. I understand you wanted to speak with me?"

The prosecutor sounded uneasy. He was probably hoping Joe wouldn't put him in a corner by turning the case into a media spectacle. Joe intended to do precisely that.

"Yes, Mr. McDonald. Thank you for returning my call. I am sure you are quite busy but I just want you to know I will be praying for you and I wish you well."

McDonald was confused. "Well, thank you for that. We, ah, all try our best here."

"Yes, yes. Of that I am sure. And I know that no matter what happens, God will judge that man. I just hope the jury sees the light and that he will never get out of prison and make another widower like me."

McDonald tried to sound tough. "Well, we both want the same thing, sir."

"Yes, yes. Of course we do. You know, those reporters kept asking me about the case, I told them that you wouldn't let me down. No sir. The Lord would give both of us strength."

"Well, I do appreciate that Mr. Haise. You can rest assured we will use every asset at our disposal in prosecuting Mr. Maxwell."

Joe thanked him again and hung up. He turned back to the online Trib and refreshed the page. Another hour went by before a quote from the State Attorney's office PR Department appeared, assuring the residents of Cook County that Mr. Maxwell would be punished to the fullest extent of the law. No resource would be spared.

Joe then dialed Al Baker, the estate lawyer. Al's secretary put the call through immediately, a privilege afforded few clients.

"Al? Joe Haise. How are things?"

"Joe, we're doing fine here. I completed an asset search, Tina's assets were all jointly held with you, so there is no need for Probate. I audited the summer camp, everything is in order and I gave appropriate authority over the charity to that young girl Julie. She was a heck of a fundraiser, your Tina. She deposited the receipts the Monday following every fundraiser. A few small checks from a medical group or law firm and a few thousand in cash just like clockwork."

Joe was getting upset again. "Yeah, well, she always got a great response when she passed the ol' hat around." Al did not seem to think the deposits were all that unusual, and Joe needed to keep this quiet until after Maxwell's trial. A large amount of cash in her purse and large cash deposits in the charity's account would be a thread that could lead to more questions by Buddy Scott and his pals.

Al interrupted Joe's train of thought. "Say, Joe, do you know a physician named Tom Phillips?"

Joe was confused. "Tom Phillips? Sure, he's my primary care physician. Why are you asking?"

"I got a courtesy call from the prosecutor's office. He said they dropped a subpoena on Phillips for some medical records."

Joe's mouth went dry. If the cops find out that he had an STD check a few days before Tina died, he was cooked. Joe was beginning to feel faint, but he steeled himself and tried to sound unconcerned. "Oh? Why would they want my medical records?"

"Oh, no. Not your records, Tina's. They figured out that he was your family physician. I'm listed as the estate attorney with the coroner's office, so they called me as a courtesy. If Tina visited that doctor, there could be something in the medical records about her, ah, relationship."

Joe breathed a sigh of relief and seized the opportunity to throw Buddy Scott a red herring to get his nose the hell out of Tom Phillips' office. "Well, she had an Ob-Gyn in Evanston. Real good doc, what was her name? Drake, I think. Yes, that's it. Gladys Drake. She would have all

123

the records. You can tell the DA to go there next." Joe knew Tina hadn't seen that doctor in four or five years, Buddy Scott would get bupkis. Now that Buddy would be thrown off the trail, Al Baker needed to go too. Al had been asking questions about some sensitive areas and Joe needed to change the subject and give him something more interesting to occupy his time.

"Listen, Al, let's go ahead and do a complete asset search for Gary Maxwell. Real estate, securities, offshore holdings, the works. Hire a private investigator if you have to. And you recall that notice of claim letter you wanted to send putting him on notice of our intent to sue for wrongful death? I think you should send it now. He's in jail, but his lawyer is there visiting him every day, I bet. And Al? Make it hurt."

Al perked up, so much so Joe thought he would jump through the phone. "You got it, Joe. After what he did to that doll of a wife of yours, we're gonna take every last nickel he has."

Joe hung up and decided he would make the last move in a week. Gary needed to stew on all of this.

Chapter 26

Joe's exercise regimen was having its desired effect and he was filling out his suits much better than before. He was getting tougher on his cases and even US Attorney Dave Dunham began calling Joe his "Old New Alpha Dog." One late summer afternoon, Joe was called to Dunham's office. He walked in and saw Financial Crimes Section head Suds Milder sitting across from Dave, Suds' eyes were red and Joe assumed he had been crying. Or he was drunk, but more likely he was crying. Dave greeted Joe warmly and asked him to sit.

"Joe, Suds and I have been talking, and he's decided to finally hang up his spurs. We both think you would be ideal to replace him as head of the Financial Crimes section of the Criminal Division."

Joe tried not to smile and donned an expression of disappointment. "Suds, I don't know what to say. No one could ever replace you." They all shook hands and talked about Suds' first days in the office. Suds cried a bit more and they all departed. Dave said he would make it official at the end of the day. Joe could not stop smiling all the way back to his office, he was ready to make a few changes.

Joe spent the rest of the afternoon refreshing his email until Dunham's email about the change came through. Not five minutes later, Jackie Dekker peered into Joe's office.

"Hey, congrats! I think The Boss make an excellent choice." She was back to wearing skirts, but the hems still stayed south of the knee and the heels were only three-quarter, but it was progress. Ellen's shadow still loomed large.

"Thanks, Jackie. That means a lot to me." Joe motioned for her to sit. "Listen, I think the work you have been doing lately is just stellar. I think you are ready for more responsibility, so I'd like you to second chair the mortgage fraud case I have."

Jackie's eyes opened wide and she thanked Joe profusely. She was so excited she could barely sit still. Joe loved every minute of it, so he took it a step farther. "Jackie, this is a big case. So let's block off Friday afternoon and we'll crank out the motion response and the witness list. We'll have our hands full, that's for sure."

Jackie didn't miss a beat and promised she'd do anything he asked. *God, I hope so,* Joe thought.

The week crawled and Joe woke up ahead of the alarm Friday morning. He took extra care getting dressed, selecting a deep red power tie and matching suspenders. He admired himself in the mirror and splashed on some new cologne he bought the day before. It was expensive but the young brunette sales clerk assured him that it drove her wild when her boyfriend wore it. That was all Joe needed to hear and he cheerfully bought the bottle.

Joe arrived at the office and sent Jackie a meeting invitation for 3:00 p.m. that afternoon. He got nothing of any substance done until his computer dinged, indicating Jackie accepted the invitation. Joe was like an excited teenager. He saw Jackie in the hallway around 2:00 p.m. She was wearing a dark sport coat and dark pencil skirt with gray stockings. The hem rested right on the knee, *maybe just a bit above it,* Joe thought. She passed by and gave Joe a smile and nod, Joe smiled back – a bit too eagerly – and noted she was wearing a camisole top under her coat. Joe wondered how toned her arms looked. *She probably has light hair on her arm, very delicate skin. Wonder what kind of lotion she uses? Or perfume for that matter? Maybe something French. She wouldn't use something one of those reality tv girls promote. No, it would be something classy.*

Just before 3:00 p.m., Joe cleared space off his desk and laid out stacks of memos and legal Reporter books. Jackie knocked at exactly 3:00 p.m. with a smile. Joe could barely contain himself and waived her in.

"Ok Joe, so what do we do?" She pulled out the chair across from Joe, he cursed himself for not arranging the chairs so she would be closer to him. She looked positively radiant, she was a vision.

"Well, let's get started with the jury instructions on Conspiracy. We need to make sure we can prove this up." Jackie sat and crossed her legs. Joe stared at her legs and his mouth quickly went dry. He adjusted his chair and tried to compose himself.

Jackie looked intensely at the binder of jury instructions, Joe looked intensely at the ivory top under her coat. He desperately wanted her to take her jacket off. "Well, let's get comfy, we'll be here a while," he offered.

Jackie continued reading and waived her hand. "I'm fine, thanks." She was almost absent-minded about it. *Didn't she want to be comfortable? I am making a real effort here and she just dismissed my genuine concern. What was her problem?*

Joe stared at her legs as the minutes passed. Joe opened a word processor and constantly spun back and forth typing broad ideas as they worked through the case. Around 5:00 p.m., Joe took a leap. "I am going to order some Chinese. Do you like pork fried rice?" Joe was proud of himself for skipping the question of whether she was hungry or had plans and went right to what she wanted to order.

"Oh, I love Chinese. Anything is great."

Joe placed the order and called the security guard with instructions. At 5:30 p.m., his phone rang and he scooted downstairs. Joe shoved money at the delivery boy and sprinted back to the elevator. He returned and Jackie hadn't moved.

"Well, let's make this a working dinner. Uncle Sam paid for this." Perk of being a Section head. Joe tried hard not to sound too important.

"I'm going to freshen up first." Jackie uncrossed her legs, stood and walked out. Joe tried to casually lean his head into her wake to smell her perfume. As she exited the main office and headed into the outer hallway, Joe ran to the far wall of his office and turned the AC down, inviting the office to slowly warm up. Jackie returned a few minutes later and Joe had a number of white cartons spread out across his desk. Jackie sat down and opened a set of chopsticks. She began devouring a carton of fried rice.

Joe watcher her scoop rice into her perfect mouth. *Did she reapply her lipstick? Maybe some gloss? That may be a signal.* She stretched her tongue out as she licked the ends of the chopsticks over and over. Joe tried to sound casual as he asked, "How's the rice?"

"Oh, it's great. You should try some." Joe reached out and snatched the carton from Jackie's hand, her finger grazed his and Joe felt a jolt go through his entire body. He eagerly scooped rice from the carton, *her carton*, and he imagined her mouth, her breath. Jackie continued to read a memo as she ate. Joe could not concentrate. He tried to focus on a brief in the middle of his desk because, at that moment, he was unable to stand up.

"Should we type some of this memo into the brief?" Jackie's eyes never left the page.

"Uh, not just now, I want to finish reading this first." Joe was beginning to sweat. He noted the room was warming up, and Jackie unbuttoned her jacket. *Please God*, Joe thought. She slipped one arm out of her coat and looked up. She caught Joe's gaze and slipped the arm back in the coat. She quickly rebuttoned the jacket and looked back at the memo.

Fine, you can sweat. Prude.

A few minutes later, Jackie seemed inspired. "Wait, I have something on Unindicted Co-conspirators in my office," she said. Jackie stood and began walking to her office; Joe was finally able to stand and followed behind her, grabbing a heavy legal Reporter book off his desk. *God, her ass is the Eighth Wonder of the World.* Jackie walked into her office and plopped in her office chair, spun away from Joe and opened a word document. Joe took the vacant seat to the side of her desk, he had a better view of her here than he had back in his office. Jackie opened a memo and spent a few minutes reading it, Joe tried to avoid getting caught staring. Jackie absentmindedly slipped out of her heels and tucked her feet underneath her thighs. Joe leaned forward and stared at her toes, tracing his gaze back up her legs to her firm hips. He moved the book onto his lap and finally gave up all pretense of not staring. His breathing quickened and he was beginning to sweat though his shirt.

Several minutes passed and Jackie made a few comments about the research. Finally, Jackie spun her chair around to face Joe and she began to stretch. "Well, I really should get going, I am starting to go buggy." Jackie unfolded her legs and stood, Joe's silent pleas for a closer look were ignored by the gods. She opened her oversized bag, pulled out a pair of flats and slipped them on.

"Sure, you need to get some rest. I'll be a few minutes behind you." Jackie thanked Joe for the Chinese food and headed for the door.

"Oh no, thank you Jackie. I think we make a great team." Joe waited for a statement of confirmation, but Jackie simply smiled and said she'd see Joe on Monday morning. *What, you don't think we make a great team? What were the last three hours about?*

Joe turned out Jackie's office light and followed her to the lobby. She waved and headed out of the main doors and walked to the elevator. Joe watched the lobby door close and listened for any sound. The office was totally silent and dark, the only light came from Joe's office. Joe walked back to Jackie's office and turned on the light. He saw her high heels lying next to her desk. He walked over, paused and checked the corridor again. Seeing no one, he quickly walked back, picked them up and held them to his nose. He inhaled deeply.

Chapter 27

Joe spent his first few days as Section head getting up to speed on whatever it was that Suds Milder did for the six hours a day he stumbled around his office. Joe concluded that Suds did two things especially well: missed briefing deadlines and spilled hobo-grade brandy on his case files. The 10% raise was apparently in exchange for spending 30 minutes per week emailing attaboys to the rest of the staff. Joe promptly declared the unit to be understaffed and convinced Dave Dunham to reassign Jackie from General Crimes to full-time in the Financial Crimes unit and finally bless Nate's transfer request. That gave Joe a compliment of Nate Maddux, himself, and Jackie. And now that Jackie worked under him, Joe decided that he could really sink his teeth into the young attorney mentoring program he was hoping to establish. Joe made a mental note to get Dave's permission to get that off the ground.

The Financial Crimes section was down two full-time prosecutor positions due to budget cuts, so they would have to make-do with current staffing levels. In order to backfill the loss, Joe Shanghaied an intern named Thomas Skinner from the Civil Division and tasked him with doing everything except trying cases. In exchange for giving Thomas a degree of responsibility over cases that bordered on the unauthorized practice of law, Joe let Thomas use Suds' old office. Joe's actions made the other interns insanely jealous as they had to scramble for whatever counter space and research projects they could find while their classmate had his own office and caseload. Eventually, one intern ultimately lodged a complaint with the Dean at the University Of Chicago Law School that Thomas was receiving too little guidance, too much responsibility and his own fully-furnished office to boot. Joe let Thomas listen in on the phone call to the

Dean that resulted in Thomas receiving a glowing mention in the student newsletter. Thomas was so grateful to Joe that he would have worn a Cubs jersey to a Sox game if Joe told him to, an act that would normally warrant a death sentence.

Joe was mentally redecorating his office when he looked up to see Nate Maddux' massive frame occupying Joe's doorway. Nate was clearly shaken, Joe had never seen him so unsteady.

"Nate? You okay?"

Nate was holding several large files and his hands were trembling. He stepped in and used his hip to close the door behind him. "Joe, I don't know what...I think I may have screwed up on the McDowell case."

Nate recently won a high-profile jury trial, it was Nate's first win of any real note and was significant enough that D.C. took notice. Dave Dunham was acutely aware that Washington was constantly on the look-out for ambitious African American prosecutors in an effort to diversify the agency. The Department of Justice nationwide had one of the highest percentages of whites of any agency in the federal government, courtesy of the hiring practices of the two previous Presidential administrations.

The McDowell case involved a road builder who bribed an Illinois State Senator to steer a combined state/federal highway contract to his company. Senator Pep McDowell built a reputation as the cleanest politician in Springfield, which is akin to claiming to be the most honest member of the Nixon administration. McDowell made an effort to help a road builder based in the Senator's district, Gorden Scott Construction, secure a $100 million contract to build an interchange on the south side of Chicago. Shortly after the contract was awarded, an anonymous tip led federal agents to raid Pep's office where they found $10,000 cash in a desk drawer. He was later charged with violating the federal bribery statute. The investigators couldn't tie the money to Gorden Scott exactly, but the company was publicly shamed into withdrawing from the contract and the runner-up, E.F. Tommasino Construction, got the contract.

Pep McDowell swore up and down that he had no idea how the money made its way into his drawer and that his efforts to help Gorden Scott, a small disadvantaged business headquartered in his district, were above-board. Dunham assigned the case to the Public Corruption Section

131

and Nate took the case and ran with it, spending hundreds of hours poring over contractor records, bank transactions and Pep's finances. Nate knew everyone was watching him and that a conviction meant instant headlines. A few more years and Nate would be poised to take a position at the Attorney General's office in Washington, D.C., possibly even an appointment to the Federal bench. But Nate had to secure the conviction first and he hadn't slept at all in the run-up to trial.

Nate had federal agents look into the banking activities of everyone involved: Pep, Gorden Scott Construction, and every other contractor who bid on the contract. Nate subpoenaed financial records for the 90-day period before the money was found in Pep's office from every bank that any contractor, or Pep, did business with in the last ten years. Despite the reams of paper from the target banks, nothing among any of them raised any red flags. However, Pep made a couple of visits to the Potawatomi Casino in Milwaukee in the weeks prior to the contract award and he was one month behind on his mortgage, which was all the jury needed to hear in order to convict. Pep didn't help his cause when he testified in his own defense and spun some elaborate tale about a massive conspiracy to sully his good name. The Chicago Trib feasted on the story, painting "Honest" Pep McDowell as just another pol in a long line of corrupt Illinois figures dating back to Governor Joel Aldrich Matteson. The entire office even held an impromptu celebration for Nate at the Exchequer when the jury came back with a guilty verdict after 89 minutes of deliberation.

Pep, of course, was forced to resign from office as soon as he was convicted. He apparently hoped the public spectacle of a teary farewell speech on the State Senate floor would help him avoid a prison sentence. Manny Pasquale monitored the trial with great interest; Manny lost to Pep by less than 500 votes two years earlier. After Pep resigned, Manny won a special election by landslide, soundly beating a registered Communist and a college student who ran for the seat as a fraternity prank.

Nate sat down and began speaking rapidly. "Joe, I was looking over the file and, you know, I was going over things for the sentencing tomorrow, you know, and there is just so much here…"

Joe interrupted Nate. "Whoa, there. Slow down, Nate. Let's just take this one step at a time."

"Okay." Nate took an exaggerated deep breath and exhaled. "I was going through the file and I found this." Nate pulled out a single page from a large stack of papers. "So, this is from the stack of banking records from all the people and companies we looked at. And you remember how hard I was working on this? Okay, I was working really hard, and there was just so much data. I remember I would come in at 7:00 a.m. and work past dinner. You know, my partner Ernest and I were going through some stuff because of all the long hours…"

Joe had never seen Nate this distressed and he was becoming concerned as well. The fact that Nate mentioned his boyfriend was a testament to his state of mind; he never mentioned his dating life at the office. Ever. "It's okay, Nate. So, what's in the bank records?" Joe gestured to the paper in Nate's hand to get him back on point.

"Okay, so, I was looking through this stack from the Farmer's Bank of Streator, and there was a note in the margin from the bank's assistant manager, Deloris something-or-other, and an arrow pointing to a line entry on the printout. And when I first saw the note, I thought it read, "EFT Conf transaction $15,000." So I assumed it was just a note that there was an EFT, or Electronic Fund Transfer, and Conf, for confirmed, for $15,000. Which doesn't really mean anything. See, but then I was looking this over and I realized I read the note wrong. See, the handwriting isn't the best, and I was working all those hours…"

"Nate? Nate? What's the problem?" Joe was leaning forward in his chair now and was unconsciously squeezing the pen in his hand.

"Well, as I looked closer this morning, I noticed the 'f' is actually an 's.' So the note reads, 'EFT Cons.' And then I realized it isn't Electronic Fund Transfer-Confirmed for $15,000, it's a cashed check from E.F. Tommasino Construction for $15,000. Just a week before the money was discovered in McDowell's office, E.F. Tommasino cashed a $15,000 check at Farmer's Bank in Streator, which is a little more than was found in the Senator's office, but still. And they end up getting the contract."

Joe was tense and he was trying to noodle out the problem Nate was laying in front of him. "Alright Nate, but why would E.F. Tommasino pay off the Senator? Gorden Scott got the contract and E.F. was the runner up. How could they get the contract anyway at that point?"

"Right. But if it was made to look like Gorden Scott paid off Mc-Dowell, then they are both out. Plus, I checked and E.F. Tommasino was the biggest contributor to Manny Pasquale in the previous election against McDowell. They didn't donate in the special election, but Manny never really had a viable challenger so it didn't matter. After Manny gets elected, E.F. gets the bid."

Joe let out a long breath. *This is a problem*, he thought. It sure looked to Joe like E.F. Tommasino arranged for money to be planted in Pep's office. *The anonymous tip. Shit. E.F. made the anonymous call, Pep's office gets searched and the money turns up, Pep gets pinched.* Gorden Scott had to withdraw from the interchange contract to avoid the appearance of impropriety and Manny was Pep's natural replacement in the State Senate. No need for E.F. Tommasino to donate to Manny's campaign this time around and draw unwanted attention; Manny had no legitimate challenger in the special election anyway. And the entire time, Nate had a note in the file that Pep's lawyers could easily use to win the trial. In fact, Dave Dunham would have dropped the charges against Pep and investigated E.F. Tommasino had he known. To make matters worse, Nate failed to hand over exculpatory evidence that was sitting in the prosecuting attorney's case file. So not only was Pep probably innocent, but Nate was looking at the ass-end of a termination hearing and possible disbarment by the Disciplinary Commission of the Illinois Bar. All because Nate failed to follow-up on a bank manager's note in the margin of a document. *Hell of a first week on the job. Why do bad things always happen to me?*

Joe needed to sort this one out, but he couldn't concentrate with Nate constantly wringing his hands and looking at Joe like a kid who got caught cheating on a test and wanted his father to call the principal and get him out of it. "Alright, Nate. Let me look at a couple of things and we can talk in the morning."

Nate began to relax, but he was still distressed. Joe decided to play this up a bit. "I don't know that I can bail you out here, Nate. But let's keep this between us for now, don't even tell Ernest, and 1 will see what I can come up with."

Nate was unable to thank Joe, he could only get out a "Tha-," and choked up. He nodded, stood up and made a bee-line back to his office.

Joe flipped open Nate's file and spent an hour reviewing its contents; Nate was sure to add every press clipping with his name in it to the file. Eventually Joe noticed that everyone in the office went home for the night. Joe wandered down to Nate's office but he already left too. Joe paced the hallway a bit and returned to his office, he cracked the file again and began to weigh his options.

Joe knew that cases involving prosecutors who were accused of failing to turn over evidence usually involved something that wasn't obviously exculpatory, but perhaps could have been used by a sharp defense attorney to blow some smoke regardless. It could be a lab test showing a third person's blood type at the crime scene, or notes from an interview of someone who was initially eliminated as a suspect; anything that can point to someone else committing the offense. But there is a pretty significant difference between a prosecutor who turns a blind eye to potentially exculpatory evidence that he or she doesn't actually have (like declining to *order* a blood test on a bloody rag), and refusing to turn over exculpatory evidence actually in your possession (like declining to *disclose* the blood test results from the bloody rag after you receive them). Failing to *discover* potentially exculpatory evidence is a civil rights violation that can lead to a conviction being reversed and the prosecutor facing formal discipline. Failing to *disclose* exculpatory evidence sitting in your own goddamn file is a career-ender. *Nate fucked up huge*, Joe thought.

But if Joe could somehow straighten this out, Nate would be ever so grateful. Hell, Nate would owe everything he had to Joe. Joe considered the evidence: it was pretty damn solid. E.F. Tommasino probably cashed a $15,000 check and paid $5,000 to the runner who planted the $10,000 bundle in the Senator's desk. Joe knew a couple of contractors who had ties to organized crime, so finding someone to get the job done wasn't that hard. There was no way Gorden Scott could stay on the job once the allegation hit the papers, even if Pep never faced formal charges. The fact that Pep was indicted, convicted, and replaced in the Senate by Manny was probably not even necessary, but it was a nice piece of insurance anyway. The sales manager, Jimmy Tommasino, was the CEO's grandson and was quoted liberally in the clippings crowing about how happy he was to take over the project from Gorden Scott. Jimmy was nowhere near the shrewd businessman his grandfather was, but what he lacked in business acumen, he more than made up for in street-smarts.

Joe had to tie up a couple of loose ends to make this work. He pulled out the page from the file with the note on it. Deloris something-or-other from Farmer's Bank of Streator must not have known how this record related to the corruption case, she hadn't called Nate or followed up in any way in 18 months. Joe was betting she was busy worrying about how market shifts affected Central Illinois soy prices and forgot about the routine inquiry from the US Attorney's office in Chicago. Most people are ecstatic when a federal prosecutor stops calling. Joe spun around to his computer, opened his browser and began searching for something almost impossible to find in the City of Chicago. Sure enough, there were still some left. He wrote the address on the back of his hand, then opened another webpage and created a dummy email account from the same website he used when he tracked Tina. Joe spun his chair back to the file, flipped through some of Nate's notes, scribbled a note on the back of his hand and closed the file. Joe then cleared his browser history, shut down his computer and headed out.

Joe drove for 15 minutes to the near south side, periodically checking the address he wrote on the back of his hand, until he spotted the nearly-extinct small silver box attached to a thin metal pole: one of the last working payphones in Chicago. Joe circled the block until he found a parking spot a block away and made his way to the phone. Joe checked up and down the block for curious onlookers, but no one paid him any attention. He approached the completely obsolete piece of equipment and decided not to think about the multitude of viruses currently breeding on the mouthpiece. Joe picked it up, poured a few quarters in the slot, looked at the number on the back of his hand and dialed. As the line rang, Joe casually scrubbed the writing off his hand and waited for an answer. It was well after 6:00 p.m., but a large company like E.F. Tommasino surely would have someone pick up after hours. Joe kept pressing 0 and let the line continue to ring until he was greeted by a live person.

"Yeah, Tommasino." The rough voice on the other end of the line was indifferent and clearly not from the customer service department. Joe surmised that the call rang through to the warehouse because he could

136

hear machines running in the background. He guessed this was the second-shift foreman.

Joe adopted something of a Bowery accent. "Yeah, get Jimmy Tomassino on the line. It's important." Joe tried to speak just above a whisper in order to convey an air of mystery.

"Ah, okay, who is this?" The warehouse foreman was already impatient.

"Look, just get him on the fucking phone. I can wait." Joe decided swearing would help create the desired effect.

"Alright, hold on." There was clearly no instruction given to the warehouse crew on gracious telephone etiquette or the proper use of the hold button, the foreman simply set the phone on a desk and walked away. Joe could hear men shouting in the background, and eventually the receiver picked up.

"Jimmy Tomassino. Who is this?"

"Jimmy, you are in a boatload of trouble. Look, I know you paid $5,000 to a runner to plant $10,000 in Pep McDowell's office." Joe paused, praying the call wasn't recorded and that his theory was actually right. If Jimmy told him to screw off, it might indicate Joe was wrong, and Nate was off the hook. If Jimmy bit, then Joe was right and he could try to clean up this mess.

"What? Fuck you, who the fuck is this? McDowell got convicted, what the fuck do you want?" Jimmy hadn't slammed the phone down yet, Joe knew his theory was right.

"Listen, Jimmy. The bad news is: I've got you cold. The good news is: I don't want anything. You just need to do one thing and you'll never hear from me again." Joe was trying to sound far more convinced of his position than he actually was.

Jimmy paused long enough to nearly stop Joe's heart before he finally said, "Are you fucking with me?"

Joe was smiling now. "Jimmy, you need to go back to your office right now, and create some dummy invoices that explain where that $15,000 went. You need to date them to the week when you set up Pep. And you need to scan and email them to this address." Joe gave Jimmy the dummy email and waited for Jimmy to say something.

137

"Okay, I got it, I got it. And what am I supposed to do then, Mister...what was your name?"

"Mr. Go Fuck Yourself, that's my name. Then you stick the invoices in a shredder, delete the sent email, and forget we ever had this fucking conversation. You have 30 minutes." Joe hung up and stared at the phone, as if it would do something. He turned and ran back to his car and drove back to the office, stopping for a burger on the way.

Joe walked into his office and unwrapped his burger while he booted up the internet. Joe took a bite, spilling ketchup on the keyboard while he checked his dummy email account. The inbox had two messages, one welcoming "Linus" to the network, and one from an account that was comprised of seemingly random numbers and letters. Joe opened the .pdf attachment and saw three crudely-crafted purchase orders, for $8,435.18, $4,212.34, and $2,352.48, which conveniently totaled $15,000. Joe knew this would never stand up to scrutiny, but it didn't have to. The standard for a prosecutor's ethical conduct was a few hundred fathoms below the professional standards for a forensic accountant. Nate just needed some-*thing* to show some*one* from the Inspector General's office, if they ever asked, why he failed to turn over the banking records to Pep's lawyers. Nate could claim his memory failed him as to where the invoices came from, but since the numbers added up, why would he need to turn the bank records over to the defense? Joe printed the invoices to his desktop printer, deleted the dummy email account and cleared his browser. He placed the invoices carefully in the back of Nate's folder. He shut out the light and headed home.

The next day Joe got to the office early; Nate was already there and pounced on Joe the moment he entered the lobby. He had been lying in wait for some time.

"Say, Joe. Any thoughts on that thing we talked about?" Nate's attempt to sound casual completely misfired. His shirt was wrinkled, he appeared to have slept in it. His eyes were puffy and he had a large cup of coffee in his hands. The expression on his face was of total desperation, pleading for Joe to get him out of the mess he was in.

"Sure Nate, come on in." Joe escorted Nate to his office, turned on his light, took off his sport coat and closed the door. Like an inspector that

138

gathers all the suspects together in a room before revealing the culprit, Joe seemed to take his time getting situated behind his desk and opened Nate's file while Nate looked desperately at Joe. "Well, I looked over the file all night Nate, and I really can't see what the problem is." Nate shot Joe a confused look, it reminded Joe of the way a dog cocks his head to the side when his owner says, "Go get me a beer, Pickles."

"Wha…what do you mean?"

"Well, Nate, it's like this. I saw the invoices from E.F. Tommasino detailing the $15,000 disbursement from their operating account. Same week that Gorden Scott paid off Pep, actually. See? Lookie here." Joe handed Nate the invoices and Nate tried to process what he was seeing. "They were right here in the file the whole time, Nate. You must have missed them. This seems to jibe with what Deloris something-or-other wrote on the statement about the cashed check. So it's all good."

Nate was distressed and looked up at Joe, who was displaying an expression of perfect serenity for Nate's benefit. Nate's eyebrows jumped as the light went on. Nate figured out what Joe did. His voice lowered to a whisper. "But, how did you…?"

"Nate, I think Senator McDowell has suffered enough. Do we really need prison time on this one? I think a modest fine is all that is required."

Nate was trying to figure out how this was supposed to work, but Joe was four moves ahead already. "But the judge will want some prison time. I mean the sentencing guidelines…"

"Well, I think a written letter from Dave Dunham, advising the judge that the US Attorney for the Northern District of Illinois strongly recommends probation, should take care of it. That will carry appropriate weight with the court."

Nate was struggling to catch up to Joe. "Um, can you…I mean, can Dave…?

"Nate, no worries. We'll get Pep to agree to waive all appeals in exchange for the probation recommendation. I'll have Dave's letter in an hour." Joe knew Dave would give him some leeway on this case; Dunham got the conviction, the headlines, and a brand new rising star in the process. He couldn't give two shits about McDowell's sentence.

Nate was clearly warming to the concept. But he furrowed his brow

139

and seemed to suffer a sudden attack of a conscience. "I don't know if I can do this, Joe. I mean, I have to represent something to the Court that I know is, um, not totally-"

Joe interrupted. "Nate, Nate, listen here. *I* don't want you to lose your license, and maybe even go to prison. And I know *you* don't want that either. And *Ernest* certainly doesn't want that. I mean, the investigation would most certainly delve into your personal life. And your grandmother, my God, what would she think when the details of your, shall we say, 'Bohemian lifestyle' come out?" Joe was exaggerating a bit for effect, but he knew Nate wasn't parsing the words that carefully. Nate put his chin down and began rubbing his massive hands over his head. A tear began running down his cheek. Nate was drowning and Joe was throwing him an anchor, now it was time to throw him a lifeline.

"Nate, don't you see the upside here? Your file is perfectly clean and there is nothing there that suggests you didn't do your due diligence. The case is done after the sentencing this afternoon, no appeals. And you know, the Attorney General's office in D.C. called asking about you last week."

Nate lifted his head, "They did?" His voice was positively buoyant.

"Oh yeah, Nate. I can't say for sure, but Judge McGill in the Central District Court in Springfield is about a year away from moving to Senior Status. I am sure they are developing a short list for that seat." Joe could tell Nate's mood was improving. Any Assistant US Attorney would cheerfully take a golf club to a cancer patient if it meant getting their name on the shortlist for a Federal judgeship.

Nate seemed to be formulating an idea. "If, ah, what if we also made sure that...?" Joe didn't want Nate trying to offer whatever in his mind qualified as "help" on Joe's masterpiece. The sentencing was in a couple hours and he didn't need Nate mucking things up now.

"It's all a done deal, Nate. You just need to finish up this afternoon. Let me handle the press. Done and done."

Nate looked more comfortable now. His posture changed and the corners of his mouth were upturned. "You know, Joe, I always thought McDowell seemed like he didn't even really want to serve in Springfield anymore. Politics seemed to exhaust him. I mean, I think we may have actually done him a favor because now he's free to, you know, try some other

140

things." Nate looked at Joe for reassurance, Joe realized Nate surrendered his moral objections quicker than a teenage girl surrenders her virginity in the backseat of a Dodge.

"Well there you go, see? If anything, McDowell is probably better off. So after we wrap up this afternoon, you can send the file off to storage, and call it an early weekend. Take Monday off if you want. But Nate, promise you'll remember us little people when you run for President." Joe and Nate both let out a laugh, but Joe wasn't completely joking. He wanted Nate to always remember this moment, when Joe saved his career. Nate stood up and shook Joe's hand. Joe gave him a reassuring squeeze on the arm and Nate walked out of the office looking like he just won the lottery, all thanks to Joe. Nate was indebted to Joe for the rest of his life.

Chapter 28

Joe went to bed that Friday evening satisfied with his performance the past week. Nate's sentencing went off without a hitch and Nate dutifully sent the McDowell file off to storage. Joe fell into a deep sleep and dreamt. In his dream he was floating down the office hall and people stood in the doorways of their offices, cheering as he passed. As Joe entered the lobby, he saw Tina sitting alone in a chair, her head down, but he couldn't see her face. *Ashamed much?* Joe asked. Tina did not respond.

Joe made it through the rest of the weekend by exercising several times each day. Monday morning came and Joe made sure he was the first one in the office. As the new Section head, he needed to set the example. Joe looked for Jackie at one point, but she wasn't in her office, yet again. *She must be busy, trying to make some progress on that mortgage fraud case,* Joe thought.

Joe wandered down the hall and spied Jackie talking to Skip Leslie, the head of the Public Corruption Section (or "The Hair", as he was known around the water cooler). He stood a good two inches taller than she did and she giggled as they talked, even tossing her hair once. Joe was unable to move and his blood pressure spiked. He was oblivious to everything around him and he suffered acute tunnel vision. He was paralyzed. Jackie and Skip were lost in conversation and Jackie nervously shifted her weight as they chatted. Jackie smiled one last time, scrunched up her face and nodded as they parted, muttering something along the lines of, "sounds great." Jackie turned and walked away smiling. Skip paused to watch her go before he finally turned and walked back to his office. Joe's hearing and peripheral vision gradually returned and he looked around frantically to see if he made a public spectacle, but no one paid him any mind. Joe stormed into his office, threw a file on the desk and fumed in his chair. Dave Dunham chose that exact moment to pop his head in and ask Joe how he was doing. Joe was in zero mood to deal with Dave.

"So, Joe. Things going well?"

"Yes, Dave. Things are fine, thanks for asking."

"Mm-hmm. Good. Good to hear. Jackie doing well?"

"Jackie?" Joe was caught off-guard. "Well, you know how it is, Dave." Joe didn't know how it is, so he decided to stall for time by asking Dave, precisely, how it is.

"Yep, yep. I hear that." Dave was trying to get to whatever point he needed to get to in the least efficient manner possible. "Skip in Public Corruption is looking to fill a spot. So, you know, there you have it."

Joe silently began grinding his teeth, Jackie's been a busy little bee. Joe decided he would have the most success quickly terminating this proposal if he talked to Dave on his level. "Well, Dave, Jackie's pretty good, but she needs a lot of polishing. Her stuff is pretty raw. So really, she needs some, you know, polishing." Joe held his cupped hands high in the air and moved them up and down slightly, as if weighing a scale. "So if you have A right here, okay, but then over here, you know, you have B. So really it could go either way there, Dave."

Dave stared into space and slowly nodded his head. "Yep, gotta get the polish there. Can't be unprepared. Big stuff happening in that Section. And this one too. Both Sections."

Dave maintained his blank stare and Joe took the offensive to end the painful encounter. "Well, thanks for stopping by, Dave."

"Oh sure. Let's, ah, you know…" Dave trailed off and wandered out of Joe's office, preoccupied with his thoughts. Joe reached for the phone, tightly gripped the receiver, and buzzed Jackie.

"Hi, Joe. What's up?"

Joe settled back in his chair and spoke through a clenched jaw. "Say there, Jackie, could you just stop by for a sec? That would be just super."

"Oh sure, I'm on my way." The line cut and Joe began silently huffing. Ten seconds later, Jackie walked in with a cheerful smile and sat. Jackie wore tight black slacks and a tissue-thin ivory top that was a tad small. Joe noted immediately that the top button on her blouse was threatening to go

143

AWOL and offer the rest of the office a peek at the troops.

Joe looked at her sternly. "Jackie, I'm looking at the memo you wrote on wire fraud, and, well, it just has a lot of holes."

Jackie's smile disappeared and she narrowed her eyes. "A lot of holes? I don't understand."

Joe refused to blink or even look away. "I didn't even ask for a memo, I just needed a citation. So your time was pretty much wasted."

Jackie's jaw dropped and Joe was certain her eyes were welling up. "But, I thought that you asked me to-"

"I can't do much with the memo, so we can stash it in the electronic archives. Or we could toss it. Either way, I suppose. Look, I simply can't tolerate you using my resources on a lark. I need to make sure your time is well-spent."

Jackie's toned shoulders stooped when Joe suggested tossing the memo, but calling her research a "lark" must have stung more than anything. It was obvious to Joe that she was desperately trying to not cry.

Joe brightened a bit and lifted the tone of his voice an octave. "But you have such talent, Jackie. Really, you are very, very good. You just need to check with me on some of this. Look before you leap, so to speak. Let's talk more often so you don't get too far over your skis."

"Thanks, I would appreciate that. I mean, I want to fit in here. I just really need this job-" Jackie cleared her throat, looked down and tried to casually use a finger to swipe the corner of her eye. Joe pretended he didn't see her dry a tear as he stood up and guided her to the door of his office. He placed his hand in the middle of her back and allowed his thumb to come to rest on her bra strap, challenging himself to locate the clasp. Jackie appeared to be too distracted trying to avoid bawling in front of her supervisor to notice, Joe simply smiled as she thanked him profusely for what she assumed were his efforts to help her career.

Joe offered a magnanimous, "Oh, you're so very welcome, Jackie."

Chapter 29

The Maxwell trial was only two weeks away and Joe was waiting for the pressure to build to some kind of resolution, but none was forthcoming. A full-blown jury trial was not an option. Joe was already hearing rumblings that Maxwell's defense team was hoping to find some kind of alternate suspect to deflect blame from Maxwell. Joe had taken to wearing a crucifix pin on his jacket, and even managed to get a nice picture of himself wearing it in the local section of the Trib. Still, he was counting on a call from *someone* asking about his thoughts on an adjournment of the trial or a possible plea deal, and the silence this close to trial was deafening. *No way this thing really goes to trial in two weeks*, Joe thought. *No freaking way.*

Maxwell's lawyer, Jack Taggart, was a well-known Chicago defense attorney. Taggart's client base was mostly white collar DUIs and the children of the Rich and Famous who got popped for possession of whatever drugs they used in Wrigleyville to get loose enough to enjoy the Cubs. He had the occasional serious felony; he represented the brother of the Bears' starting tackle on a child porn charge. He was in the news for a solid week and the acquittal was worth another two years' worth of clients. The fact that Jack arranged for his client's brother to sit in court during the Bears' playoff run probably didn't hurt.

Joe learned that Jack spent the morning in court arguing a motion to dismiss based on religious grounds. His client, the Right Reverend Lionel James, pastor of the fourth largest predominantly black church in the Midwest, had a disagreement in the church rectory. His secretary insisted she was pregnant with his baby, Reverend James was certain it was the first Immaculate Conception in two thousand years. The Devil forced him to throw a lamp at her head (allegedly) and the Rev. failed to understand why

145

forgiveness and redemption weren't codified in the Illinois criminal code. The hearing did not go well.

Joe suspected Taggart would not have made it back from court yet but he telephoned his office anyway. He left a short message to Jack: *Joe Haise calling, please call back.* Joe figured Jack was not unaccustomed to the occasional threatening phone call from a relative of a victim, but he knew Jack would view this differently. Joe knew Gary Maxwell wanted to shift the blame to the grieving husband, a strategy Jack likely resisted. Joe also guessed that Jack asked an investigator to find another suspect, any suspect, and someone was poking around Joe's life. Joe had nothing concrete, but a few telephone hang-ups and a car driving past his house at odd hours made him uneasy. It could have been garden variety paranoia, but he didn't want to take a chance. Joe sat in his office and waited for the return call.

He grew tired of waiting and sauntered down to Stacey's desk. Stacey Wozniak took over for Ellen and because Joe had no small hand in her selection, and she was eternally grateful for his efforts. She was a short, bubbly thing with cropped black hair, a large chest and a flair for sexually-charged banter. She was not especially bright but she knew how to follow orders and was too insecure to challenge authority, qualities that endeared her to Joe.

"Hey Stace! How was your weekend?" Joe casually leaned on her desk, trying to catch a glimpse down her blouse.

"Ohmygod! So me and my friends Laurie and Kayla went out and it was re-dunculous! These guys bought us shots of tequila, and like, I can *not* handle tequila. But Kayla was all like, 'Stacey, these guys are totally cute.' So I was like…"

Joe stared at her chest and tuned out her voice. *God, she is dim.* Joe wondered whether she had sex with a different guy every night. *She probably did. Slut.* Joe interrupted her stream-of-consciousness rant.

"Yeah, so, listen Stacey. I need to keep close contact with the folks in my Section. You know, we do some pretty sensitive stuff, so I need to stay in touch. So I am going to need basic information for Jackie Dekker, Nate, that intern Thomas, and you, of course."

Stacey lit up at the mention of "sensitive stuff" and her name. Gossip was her drug of choice and Joe was offering to be her supplier.

146

"Ohmygod! Absolutely. I can get you all that."

"Great, just great. I need home address, cellphone number, if we have personal email too, that would be great, just great."

Stacey was beaming and offered to get the information immediately. Joe acted casual and told her that the end of the day would be fine. Joe returned to his office and crafted an email to Nate, Jackie, Thomas and Stacey.

To: <Maddux, Nate; Dekker, Jackie; Skinner, Thomas; Wozniak, Stacey>

From: <Haise, Joseph>

Cc: <Empty>

Bcc: <Empty>

Subject: <Contact Info.>

Welcome to the team! I am so pleased to be working with each of you. I want to be available 24/7 in case you ever need me. We are going to be working on some sensitive cases and I never want personal security to be a concern. My personal cellphone is at the bottom of this email, you can reach me anytime. I will send a text message to each of you later confirming I have the most up-to-date contact information. Thank you and let's go get 'em!

Joe decided the last sentence would be his new catchphrase. The two desk Sergeants in Hill Street Blues each had a catchphrase, Joe felt he needed one too. He sat back in his chair, pleased with himself when the phone rang.

"Joe Haise, Section Chief." Joe added the title, no other section chief did so but Joe felt he had earned it.

"Joe, Jack Taggart." Joe began to speak, but Jack cut him off. "Listen, Joe, I know you know the rules. If you are calling about the civil claim, I have to deal with Al Baker. And if you want to talk about the criminal trial, you really should let the Victim/Witness coordinator know that you want to talk to me."

Joe knew Jack was dying to talk to him, but needed to cover his ass with the Illinois Bar by making the disclaimer.

"Understood Mr. Taggart." Joe would offer no such first-name informalities, he was a grieving husband talking to the man who was defend-

147

ing her killer. Or something like that. "As a member of the Bar, I know the ethics code as well. I just wanted to know if your client was intending on going to trial in two weeks."

Joe was positive he could actually hear Jack stiffen in his chair. "We're going to do what we need to, Joe. I am sure you can appreciate my situation here. You should know my client is adamant he did not do this thing to your wife. Your late wife, I mean. Tina, that is."

Joe could sense Jack was not especially convinced of his client's innocence. He decided to strike. "Well, Mr. Taggart, I know what the evidence looks like. And I've been prosecuting for over a decade and I know a slam dunk when I see one. But as a Christian, I also believe in the importance of family. Your client's wife and twin girls, for example."

"Well, Mrs. Maxwell has already retained a divorce lawyer, Joe."

"Oh, Lord. Those dear children. The bonds of marriage are sacred." Joe tried his best to sound sincere, Jack Taggart was confused.

"Um, yes. Of course. Sacred bonds."

"You see, Mr. Taggart, Tina was too fine a woman to have any real enemies. I am convinced your client did not mean to hurt her. He may have lost his temper in an instant."

Taggart was beginning to get interested. "Yes, I see."

"Yes, yes. And I don't want those kids going to college with their father behind bars, unable to pay their tuition. Constantly struggling. How does a life sentence and bankruptcy filing help those girls?"

Taggart was sipping coffee and almost spit it out. The girls were six, was Haise suggesting he would sign off on a 10-12 year deal? That meant a plea to Murder 2. Pay tuition? Was he saying he'd deal on the civil claim? Taggart stammered. "We…well, they are six now, and I am not sure that Gary would, ah, *allocate* in such a fashion that, ah, you or the prosecutor may, ah, require for these charges. And certainly the children's well-being is foremost in his mind."

Jack was struggling to send Joe a message. Ethically, none of the attorneys could tie a civil settlement and a criminal settlement together, but with sufficient back-channel innuendo, it could be done. Based on Taggart's not-too-subtle hint, Joe deduced that he needed to lean on the DA so Maxwell could nail down an Alford plea, which is a plea of guilty coupled with a denial of responsibility. A Guilty plea is when a defendant says, "I did it." A No Contest plea is when a defendant says, "Meh. I ain't saying I did it, and I ain't saying I didn't do it. All I'm saying is, I know I'm gonna lose the goddamn trial." But an Alford plea is altogether different. A defendant invoking an Alford plea is really saying, "Yeah, sure, I plead guilty, Your Honor. But just between us, I didn't really do it." In any sensitive case where a prosecutor refuses to allow a No Contest plea to satisfy the masses' demand that someone accept responsibility for the crime, an Alford plea is an easy sell. The prosecutor gets to hear the word, "Guilty," and the defendant doesn't have to actually admit to anything. Joe knew Maxwell obviously couldn't describe to the court precisely how he killed Tina, but Joe needed the plea regardless. And agreeing to a modest cash settlement should sweeten the deal.

Joe sounded appropriately concerned. "Yes, yes, of course. Certainly a trial would be so very difficult. Especially on those little girls. And that lovely wife of his." Joe recalled pictures in the paper of Maxwell's trophy wife. She appeared to own nothing but yoga pants and jog bras. Probably walked around the house dressed like that. Joe began to wonder if she would find a man like him attractive. He refocused and hit Taggart with both barrels.

"Well, Mr. Taggart, Bill McDonald and I have talked and I am ready to testify, if need be. And I think you should know something of critical importance."

"And what's that, Joe?"

"Tina and I had a talk a week before she died. You see, Tina had difficulties getting pregnant. She cried and I held her. God had a different plan, I suppose, because she would have been such a wonderful mother, so we decided to adopt a child from China. A little girl, as a matter of fact. Tina would have been such a great role model for a young girl. he shared her gifts with so very many, and I think many more were deprived of her…talents…far too soon." Joe wished someone could appreciate his innuendo. "I have asked God for support when I testify, I fear I will need the strength of Job to manage. Oh yes, the strength of Job."

"Well, ah, Joe, I thank you for, ah, sharing that." Taggart was thrown. Joe knew he was trying to calculate how to deal with Joe as a witness, and what the jury would do with that kind of devastating testimony. If Joe came across as sincere on the stand as he did on the phone, the jury would simply stop the trial halfway through and declare that Maxwell was a guilty sonofabitch who deserved to hang. Joe knew Taggart was now frantically thinking of a relatively painless way to avoid trial. They exchanged good-byes and Joe hung up. The chess pieces were moving into place.

Chapter 30

Joe waited until the end of the week before attempting another maneuver. The office had settled into a routine, Joe actually had quite a bit of work to do and was not able to mentor Jackie as much as he'd hoped. He sensed people were avoiding him as the murder trial approached, assuming he was on edge. He began having troubling dreams at night. He kept seeing Gary Maxwell, silently leering at him in court.

Friday arrived and the trial was ten days away, Joe had not heard a peep since he talked to Taggart earlier in the week. He was getting anxious and needed to get things moving. He was considering his next play when the phone rang. Joe picked it up and was greeted by a young woman's voice.

"Mr. Haise? This is Alicia with the Victim/Witness office. Mr. Mc-Donald would like you to come down on Monday for trial prep. Are you available at 2:00 p.m.?"

Joe grimaced. *Trial prep? What the hell is he doing? I laid out a path to a plea deal and the idiot DA can't see it? He thinks his case is so strong that he can refuse to consider a plea deal? He really wants to risk a jury trial? Fine. He needs help? I'll help.*

"2:00 p.m. is fine. Tell Mr. McDonald I'll be there."

Joe hung up and stewed in his office the rest of the afternoon. He plotted how he would deal with this new twist, not reaching any particular conclusion. Around 4:30 p.m. he was getting too irritated to sit and began to pace around his office. Joe decided to pay Jackie a visit. He sauntered down the hall, only a few people still lingered around the office this late on a Friday. He turned the corner to Jackie's office and was confronted with… no one. She already left. *Did she have a date or something?* Joe cursed under his breath, and stormed out.

He returned to his office and sat in his chair while his mood soured. His concentration was broken when Nate Maddux walked past his office and leaned his head in.

"You're the last one, Joe."

"Thanks, Nate. I'll put the cat out before I go."

Nate cocked his head momentarily then began to laugh as he turned and headed to the door. Joe heard the ding of the elevator and then silence. Joe realized for the first time since last week, the office was totally abandoned. He quickly stood and walked to the door. He peered out and checked the halls, one light glowed from the copy room. Joe quickstepped down the hall and peeked in. Seeing no one, he straightened up and walked with purpose to Jackie's office.

Joe paused as he entered and surveyed Jackie's world. He knew at that moment that everything in her office was under his authority. Her job, her chair, everything in her desk, those high heels, he was in charge of it all. He put his hand over the light switch and paused, leaving the room dark. Joe walked to her desk and looked at the display. A framed picture of Jackie and some random guy was on the right-hand side, Joe had not seen that before, it must have been new. *Could be her brother, they aren't hugging or anything.* Joe noticed her black heels lying on the floor under her desk, he looked down and drew a slow smile. He began opening her desk drawers, but found only office supplies. He was, however, impressed with the order and cleanliness of it all. Unlike Tina, who wallowed like swine with any man with $1,500 to spare and brought disease and filth into their bed, Jackie was neat and tidy. She did not seem the type to spread her legs for just anyone. Joe was certain of that.

He opened the bottom drawer and hit the mother lode. Joe bent over and snatched up a small purple sachet that contained a bottle of her perfume. Coco by Chanel. Joe spritzed the air and allowed the scent to wash over his face. He hunkered down, stuffed the perfume in the sachet and carefully placed it back in the drawer. He rifled past a small lipstick case and took inventory: hair brush, nail file, a bottle of drug store hand lotion and a few Luna bars. Joe spotted something white in the back and reached in and pulled out a pair of Jackie's worn running socks. The air was sucked from Joe's lungs and he could barely contain himself. He parted his lips

152

and brought the treasure up to the tip of his tongue.

Jackie's office light lit up the room and Joe stood up so quickly he banged his knee on the desk drawer. He dropped the socks back in the drawer and spun around in a panic. He was confronted by a startled young woman from the cleaning service.

"What the fuck are you doing?!" Joe screamed. Joe's face felt flush and his heart rate shot through the roof.

"Oh, I am so sorry mister! I am so sorry!" The young Hispanic woman had a thick accent and was clearly more terrified than Joe.

"I was just trying to grab a file here, you stupid bitch!" Joe fumbled around Jackie's desk for anything remotely resembling a file and held aloft the first thing he found.

"Oh, sir! I did not know anyone was still here!"

Joe's breathing began to normalize but he noted that she was still terrified. He displayed his most menacing gaze and was about to make some kind of threat when a vacuum cleaner roared somewhere down the hall. Joe exhaled and quickly brushed past the young woman. "Well, just be more careful! People are still working here, you know," he barked.

Joe went back to his office, calmly composed himself, and headed home for the weekend.

Chapter 31

Monday came and Joe was a week away from trial. He managed to get little work done and left the office at 1:30 p.m. to head to the Cook County State's Attorney's office for his trial prep. Joe spent the weekend rehearsing and was as ready as he was going to be. He took special care getting dressed, selecting a bright yellow tie and a cheery light blue suit he hadn't worn in years. He arrived at the office, parked and checked in at the front desk with the receptionist and waited. A minute later, a twenty-something flamboyant young hipster emerged, complete with sandals and black rimmed glasses that may or may not have contained lenses. He introduced himself as "Chet" and escorted Joe back to a small room. Bill McDonald was waiting and stood to greet Joe, and the three sat down on cheap plastic folding chairs around a small green metal table.

"Mr. Haise, good to finally meet you in person." Bill McDonald was Gabe Kaplan's long-lost brother. He had frizzy black hair and wore an off-white short sleeve button-down shirt and a light brown tie, brown slacks and cordovan shoes. Joe couldn't help but think someone from Hollywood called Central Casting and ordered up one bureaucrat. Bill sat back down and pulled out a file with "Haise, J." written on it. Joe craned his neck in order to make out the names on several other files, including Buddy Scott, the coroner Dr. Thomas Czewski, and Anthony Cayhill. Joe remembered from somewhere that was the name of the newspaper kid who caught Maxwell in his driveway that morning.

"Mr. Haise, I want to go over your testimony for the trial next week. I know you have quite a bit of experience with your background, so I don't think we need to head over to the courthouse for a full mock examination. I usually only do that with civilian witnesses." McDonald winked and gave Joe a knowing smile. The idea that Bill McDonald considered himself Joe's colleague almost made Joe laugh. *I'm a Federal prosecutor, this clock-puncher couldn't carry my briefcase.*

"I think I can manage, Mr. McDonald. So, any idea if this Maxwell character is going to beg for some kind of deal? My probate lawyer has been in touch with his lawyer regarding any possible claim for my late wife's estate. Just so you know."

McDonald waived his hand, seemingly disinterested. "Oh, well, I am supposed to meet with the defense attorney tomorrow to discuss some pretrial matters, the order of witnesses and such. We'll see what he has to say." McDonald made little eye contact with Joe as he talked, instead concentrating on making notes in Joe's file. Joe could barely conceal his contempt. "Now, Mr. Haise, we'll go over some basic questions, and I will try to prepare you for cross-exam. So let's run through this as if you're on the stand."

Joe sat back in his chair, folded his arms across his chest and smiled. "Shoot."

McDonald screwed up his face into something resembling intensity and he tried to assume a more serious tone. He was now lord of the theater, performing for a jury of Chet. Joe did his best not to laugh at the exercise, McDonald was no threat to join the Bard anytime soon. "Mr. Haise, tell me about Tina. What kind of person was she?"

Joe spoke slowly, pausing every few seconds as if searching for the right words. "Well, let's see...she was short...not very tall, really. Also, she had dishwater blonde hair, although it gets more honey blonde in the summer, and she usually wore her hair in a bun. But also, sometimes-"

McDonald interrupted. "No, what I mean is, what kind of person was she? See, I ask these questions to give the jury some idea of what Maxwell took from you. From all of us."

Joe's face lit up like a Buddhist who just found enlightenment. "Ohhh, sure, sure. I get you now." Joe straightened up in his chair and shook his hands out like a Broadway actor prepping for a scene. He looked McDonald in the eye, and with all the intensity he could muster, leaned forward and said, "Well, let me tell you, she was real nice. Just a real nice person." Joe paused for several seconds then broke character. He

155

smiled and winked at Chet as if truly pleased with himself. "Is that what you mean, Mr. McDonald?"

McDonald sighed, removed his glasses and he pinched the bridge of his nose. "Well, Mr. Haise, if you can just speak from the heart a bit more. Just let us know how you feel." He replaced his glasses and focused on Joe.

"Oh, sure. Okay, I got you now." Joe cleared his throat, removed all expression from his face and stared at McDonald for a full ten seconds without flinching. McDonald became visibly uncomfortable and Joe could sense that even Chet was uneasy. Finally, when the silence became unbearable, Joe looked around the room confused. "You mean right now?"

"Yes, now. I mean, no. Well, I'll tell you what. Let's try some other ones." McDonald was paying closer attention now and was writing more in Joe's folder. Chet shifted in his chair. McDonald flipped another page of his notes and looked at Joe with measure of concern now. He cleared his throat and spoke more forcefully. "Mr. Haise, in the weeks and months leading up to her death, did your late wife have any enemies? Anyone who wished her harm?"

Joe leaned back, folded his hands on his knee and shook his head. "Oh Lord, no. She was a peaceful, loving woman. She just loved everybody. Really, I mean absolutely everybody. In fact, I am having a hard time imagining why anyone would want to just choke her like...like...like... some kind of chicken." McDonald fumbled the file, nearly dropping it, while Chet spit out some of his Evian. But Joe didn't so much as bat an eye, causing McDonald and Chet to look at each other and carry on as if Joe didn't understand his own gaffe.

Bill adjusted his tie. "Alrighty, then. Moving on. Mr. Haise, tell us about the last time you saw Tina."

Of course, Bill. See, I was strangling the dimwit in some asshole's driveway. "Well Mr. McDonald, let me think. I remember she left that morning for work and then she was going to care for her mother in Peoria that night. See, her mother has a bad hip and Tina occasionally spent the night in Peoria caring for her." Joe stared at his shoes and began stroking his chin. "Or, I guess, she said she was spending the night in Peoria." Joe looked up instantly. "But now I suppose she was sleeping with the other fellow

156

instead the whole time."

McDonald jumped in. "Ye...well, no. I mean, you can tell the jury about what she told you, about where she was going that night. But we can fill in all the other stuff later." McDonald was getting frustrated.

Joe looked at Bill quizzically and nodded. "Oh, sure Bill." Joe was biting his cheeks to keep from smiling at this point. McDonald began flipping pages in the folder more quickly and shifted in his chair.

"Mr. Haise, were you aware your wife was having some kind of... relationship with Mr. Maxwell?" McDonald eyed Joe closely while Chet uncrossed his legs and stiffened in his chair.

Joe tried to look wounded as he spoke. "Mr. McDonald, I loved my wife. And she wasn't perfect. Not by a mile." McDonald seemed to relax a bit. "But certainly I can understand that she had needs. You know, I think the Lord gave her those urges to test her. Mr. Maxwell too. And I cannot blame them for having those urges. I mean, if two people are, you know, *together*, for example. And then they start having relations, you know, oral and whatnot-"

McDonald practically leapt out of his chair and was already standing up before Joe even finished his sentence. "Okay, Mr. Haise, why don't we take a break? Can Chet get you some water?"

"Oh, that would be divine." McDonald closed his file, tucked it under his arm, and left the room with Chet in tow, slamming the door behind him. Joe got up and pressed his ear to the door. He could hear the two in the hallway talking rapidly, but all he could make out was Bill telling Chet, "We're fucked."

Chapter 32

It was midweek, the trial was set for the following Monday. Joe returned to his office from a meeting and saw the red light on his phone, indicating he had a message in his voicemail inbox. Joe entered his passcode and heard Al Baker's panicked voice begging Joe to call him back. Joe guessed that by now, Jack Taggart had called Al and advised him that Joe called him directly and hinted at some kind of minimal cash settlement. Joe sat back and smiled, Al was pissed because his fee was a standard 1/3 contingency. And 1/3 of $30 million is a hell of a lot better than 1/3 of, say, $300,000. But Al would get over it. Joe would quote the Bible about forgiveness or something and Al would bite his tongue and collect his $100,000 fee. The call also suggested to Joe that a plea deal was in the works with Bill McDonald; Jack Taggart would not have bothered calling Al Baker if he wasn't about to wrap up the civil and criminal cases together. Joe waited for Bill McDonald to call him and break the news. Joe stared at his phone, grinning like the cat that ate the canary.

Within half an hour, his phone rang. Joe let it go a few times and picked up. It was McDonald.

"Mr. Haise, Bill McDonald. Say, listen, there are some developments in the Maxwell case I need to share with you." He sounded gravely concerned.

"Oh? What happened Mr. McDonald?" As he spoke, Joe was moving the mouse around his computer screen, shooting for a personal best in Minesweeper.

"Well, Mr. Haise, it's like this. And being a prosecutor, I am sure you appreciate my situation here. The defense is quite sure they can get a full acquittal. See, no one actually *saw* Mr. Maxwell commit the murder. And he lawyered up immediately at the murder scene, so we don't have any incriminating statements we can use. We also really don't have much of a motive either. No one heard an argument, she had no bruising on her body, and there is no indication their relationship was unstable. And forensics really adds nothing to the case, no DNA, no prints, nothing. In the end, we have no eyewitnesses, no confession, no physical evidence, and a weak motive based on what we can only assume was an argument between two lovers that turned violent. Now, *you* know and *I* know that the case is whatever we, as prosecutors, can do with it."

Joe couldn't believe Bill McDonald was trying to hustle him. Joe considered challenging him to actually prosecute this pile-of-shit called a murder trial, but he ultimately decided McDonald was so spineless that he might actually goad him into doing precisely that, so he surrendered. Joe clicked a square on the computer monitor and a cartoon mine exploded, killing his icon and ending his quest for a high score. "Goddamn it."

"Oh, I understand your concern, Mr. Haise. I am upset too. And Sergeant Scott is beside himself over this deal, but that's another story. See, if Maxwell goes through with a trial, he's 50/50 to get convicted. And I really just want him off the street for a while. You and I are in a tough business, Mr. Haise."

You would piddle all over your sensible cordovan shoes if you had to handle a federal case, pal. "Yes, yes, of course. Tough business. So what can we do, you and I, to keep him off the streets? If only for a while?"

"Well, I really squeezed Mr. Taggart. Told him I could get 25 years if I win the trial. He buckled immediately and begged for a 5-year deal. I told him I would offer him Second Degree Murder, 10-12 years. I would settle for nothing less. Mr. Haise," McDonald paused for effect, "He took it."

There was a better statistical chance that the Cubs will win the World Series in this millennium than there was that the conversation actually took place as McDonald described it. Taggart and McDonald probably engaged in a 30-second dick-measuring contest and then said, "Murder 2, 10-12 years" at the same time. *Fucking cowards.*

"Oh! Mr. McDonald!" Joe tried to sound like a teenage girl that just got a new car from her daddy. "You really did that? I can't believe it! How can I ever thank you?"

McDonald could not conceal his pride and continued to gloat like Superman patting the head of grateful little boy. "Well, Mr. Haise, just doing my job." *Magnanimous prick.* "Just be sure you are there Monday for the plea and sentencing. The judge will ask you if you wish to make a statement. It's up to you whether you do so."

Joe thanked him again profusely and hung up. He looked around his office and marveled at his universe, he was so close now. *Can't get complacent here, it ain't over yet,* he thought. Joe had seen too many cases that were supposedly a done deal, only to turn sideways at the last minute.

Joe's third or fourth trial, he couldn't recall which, he and the defense attorney reached an oral agreement a week before the jury pick. It was a small check forgery case, worth about $1,000. But one of the victims was a Congressman's kid, so the case got the federal treatment. The defense attorney, "Loophole" Louie Kryczek, Joe later learned, spent more time appearing before the Illinois Disciplinary Commission than he did appearing before any Federal District Judge. Joe did what any rookie lawyer would do when you reach an agreement with a colleague that you don't know is a complete shyster - he cut all his witnesses loose, cleared his calendar, and even scheduled a long-overdue dentist appointment for that afternoon.

The morning of trial, Joe arrived at court with a thin manila folder and not a care in the world; Loophole Louie stood and announced that he and his client were prepared for jury selection. Joe practically screamed, "But he told me we had a plea agreement!" Naturally, Kryczek feigned ignorance and the judge shot Joe the same disapproving look that an owner gives a puppy that just shit on the carpet. The judge took pity on Joe. They adjourned for the day after *voir dire* and the jury pick and Joe spent all night pulling witnesses from across Illinois. The US Attorney at the time, Dave Dunham's predecessor, just laughed and told Joe it was a "teachable moment."

The Maxwell case would not be over until Judge Holmes accepted the plea and handed down the sentence. Only then could Joe haul ass out of that County Court cesspool back to the ornate trappings of the Federal judiciary.

Chapter 33

Joe skipped going to the office completely the morning of the plea. He woke early and spent an hour picking out a dark suit with a dark blue tie. He shined up his crucifix pin and affixed it to his lapel, then spent a few minutes rehearsing his "grieving husband" look in the mirror. He practiced muttering under his breath, but just loud enough for any nearby reporter to hear, "Lord, help me...Lord, help me." Joe knew there was a sin in the Bible somewhere about using Jesus' name like this, but since Man is imperfect, Joe figured God would let him slide on this one. He satisfied himself, shut off the bathroom light and headed to the car.

Joe arrived at court and nodded soberly to the handful of reporters in attendance. He caught a glimpse of Buddy Scott sitting in the gallery, leering at Joe. Joe was transfixed by Buddy's glare and couldn't move, Buddy was clearly bothered about something and was burning a hole through the back of Joe's head. It was as if he wasn't buying whatever Joe was selling. Joe was immediately buttonholed by Chet, who was wearing a sport coat and slacks, both a size too small, finished off with brown loafers and white socks. Joe could swear Chet gave off a faint odor of marijuana. He nervously guided Joe through a door next to the jury box in the back of Judge Holmes' courtroom. It led to a small room with a solid metal table and a few chairs. There was a large metal ring attached to the table and another on the floor under the chair. The room smelled like a combination of cleanser, urine and vegetable soup. Joe hated County Court, it was beneath him.

Chet looked terrified, his tie was askew and his voice cracked as he spoke. "Mr. McDonald will be here shortly, Mr. Haise. But we are all set to go."

Joe was a little on edge, he was not going to relax until Maxwell pled. "Fine, thanks." Joe could hear rustling outside in the courtroom. He knew the media was getting set up and the court personnel were all fixing their hair and practicing their speeches. Federal judges did not allow t.v. cameras in their courtrooms, it was a much more dignified atmosphere than this circus.

Moments later, a clerk knocked on the door and peered in. "We're ready Chet."

Chet stood and nearly tripped over his feet. He said in a rushed voice, "Okay, Mr. Haise, let's go!" *You could use some more weed*, Joe thought.

The courtroom was packed but the first seat behind the prosecutor was vacant and a small white sign on the bench announced that it was "Reserved by the Victim/Witness office." Chet guided Joe to that space, Joe tried to look appropriately dour as he took his seat. Gary Maxwell was already seated at the defense table in an orange jumpsuit, surrounded by two Cook County Sheriff's Deputies. This was a good sign. If something was wrong with the plea deal, Maxwell would be in a crisp suit in case they needed to proceed to trial. The entire front row behind Maxwell was empty. The soon-to-be ex-wife and daughters must have elected to attend to other matters this day. Taggart was seated next to Maxwell and was reviewing his notes. McDonald was at his table doing the same. The court clerk, seated at a desk in front of the judge's bench, was looking back over her shoulder to see if the judge was ready. Gary Maxwell was looking directly at Joe. Joe struggled not to meet his gaze. *Not going to give you the satisfaction, you prick. Hope my wife was worth it. Don't bend over for the soap.*

The clerk turned back to the gallery and she nodded to the bailiff. He straightened up. "All rise! Court for the Honorable Terrance Holmes is now in session. Draw near and you shall be heard." The entire courtroom rose at once, and the only sound was Judge Holmes walking to the bench.

Judge Homes was clearly suppressing a smile, a high-profile case was the mother's milk of local elected judges. So long as he didn't screw it up, it was a guaranteed reelection. He took his seat at the bench and spoke. "Be seated. Madame Clerk, call the case."

As the audience in the courtroom retook their seats, the clerk opened a file and stood. "People of the State of Illinois versus Gary Max-

162

well, Murder in the First Degree. Appearances?"

McDonald, once again wearing some god-awful earth toned suit, stood. "Bill McDonald for the State of Illinois, your Honor."

Taggart, wearing a suit that clearly cost more than Joe made in a week, slowly rose, as if he was about to part the Red Sea. "Jack Taggart appearing on behalf of Gary Maxwell, who is present in the courtroom."

Judge Holmes nodded to the attorneys and opened his file. "I see we are on for a jury pick this morning, but my clerk informs me there has been a development."

McDonald cleared his throat, but Taggart stole the moment and interrupted before he could even speak. "Your honor, Mr. McDonald and I have reached a plea agreement and we will place that on the record this morning and proceed directly to sentencing."

The courtroom immediately buzzed. Joe stared straight ahead, Maxwell shifted his gaze and was now staring directly at the judge.

"Very well. Mr. McDonald, what are the terms of the plea?"

"Judge, the State will amend the charge to Murder in the Second Degree, and upon a plea of Guilty to the charge, the State will recommend a sentence of 10-12 years in the Illinois State Prison system."

The courtroom buzzed again, and the judge began to get annoyed with the distractions. "Fine, fine. Mr. Taggart, is that your understanding?"

Taggart rose, "It is your Honor, with one clarification. My client will actually enter an Alford plea."

Joe tensed up. Some judges will refuse to accept an Alford plea to some charges. If the defendant is charged with beating his wife, for example, most plea agreements require anger management counseling. If the defendant is pleading guilty to get the deal, but won't admit that he actually beat his wife, counseling is pointless. Joe wasn't sure what Judge Holmes would do with an Alford plea to Murder 2.

"I see." Judge Holmes spent a minute reading the court file. The mood in the courtroom turned tense. Judge Holmes closed the file, looked up at the attorneys, and said, "Very well, then. Let's proceed." *What a wimp,* Joe thought. *You'd never survive as a federal judge.*

McDonald recited the factual basis from the complaint. He droned on about "...certain issues that remain unresolved..." regarding details of the offense, a veiled reference to proof problems so the judge would understand why they reached a plea deal. But the courthouse is a small place and Holmes probably knew the unpublished details of the case as well as anyone. After ten minutes, McDonald concluded, saying, "For these reasons, we are willing to accept a plea to the terms afore described."

The judge turned to Taggart. "Is that a correct recitation, Mr. Taggart?"

"Well, the factual portion of the complaint is, ah, something we don't necessarily agree with 100%, obviously. But there are sufficient facts to support the Alford plea and we urge Your Honor to accept the agreement."

Judge Holmes nodded and ordered Maxwell to stand. Taggart stood and helped his client navigate the handcuffs and shackles as he stood. Maxwell looked Holmes directly in the eye, showing no expression at all.

"To the charge of Murder in the Second Degree, Mr. Maxwell, how to you plead?"

"Alford, Judge."

Judge Holmes did a double-take and Taggart immediately whispered in Maxwell's ear. Maxwell looked back at the judge. "I mean, Guilty, your Honor."

Joe bit his cheeks in an effort to suppress his smile. But out of the corner of his eye, Joe noticed that Buddy Scott looked down at his notes and shook his head in a display of disapproval. Joe removed a handkerchief and wiped the sweat from his brow. Judge Homes cleared his throat. "Very well, you understand you are pleading guilty and I will find you guilty. I will not ask you to allocute to the details of the offense because of your Alford plea. And I am free to sentence you to 20 years in the Illinois State Prison if I want. Do you understand that?"

"Yes, sir." Maxwell still showed no emotion.

"Very well. I find that you are of sound mind and are entering this plea voluntarily. I hereby find you guilty of Murder in the Second Degree and order a conviction be entered in the record. I understand the parties have stipulated to the waiver of a presentence report and we may proceed directly to sentencing. Mr. McDonald?"

Joe let out an audible sigh. *Halfway home.* Maxwell retook his seat as

Bill McDonald introduced a written statement from Julie, the cute grad student now running the Her Way camp. Joe made a mental note to stop by her office for a personal visit later on, perhaps he could help her with some of the legal formalities of the camp. Or at least take her out for drinks to get her up to speed. McDonald read the statement slowly, and Joe decided it was long-winded. Julie talked about how Tina loved the camp and the girls. She described how she worked to exhaustion but that she seemed to assume a motherly role for girls who often did not have a functioning mother in their lives. Joe remained stoic. Bill then read a letter from Tina's mother, who was too devastated to attend, and has not spoken to Joe in months. Midge wrote about how she and Tina spent so much time together, how Tina really had few if any close friends growing up, and about Tina's dreams of becoming a ballerina. Joe tuned out the prosecutor.

McDonald than turned to Joe, and said, "Your Honor, the victim's husband has a few words, I think."

The courtroom grew tense and everyone looked at Joe. On cue, Joe rose, slowly walked through the waist-high swinging gate separating the attorneys from the audience, and walked to the prosecution table while Bill McDonald moved a vacant chair in place next to him. Joe sat down as McDonald slid a microphone across the table and proudly sat back, folded his arms across his chest and flashed the television cameras a reassuring smile, as if he was telling his son to show off a new magic trick in front of the neighbors. *Putz*, Joe thought.

Joe pulled a piece of paper from his jacket, making sure no one could see its contents. He deliberately reached for an empty glass, poured some water from the pitcher on the table, and took a long drink. Every courtroom observer held their collective breath as Joe set the glass down and spoke.

"Your Honor, thank you for the time. And I want to thank Mr. McDonald here for bringing a painful matter to a more humane conclusion." McDonald flashed a smug smile, Joe struggled to keep from shoving his rayon tie into his obnoxious mouth. "I also want to thank Mr. Taggart over there. I understand he is in a difficult position. And I think the sentence everyone has been talking about is fair." Joe unfolded the piece of paper and looked down at its contents. "You see, my Tina..." Joe's voice trailed off

165

and he paused for nearly a minute. He finally shook his head and stood, walking back to his seat next to Chet, as if too devastated to continue. Joe quickly shoved the completely blank piece of paper back in his pocket and waived off Chet's monumental concern for Joe's well-being.

The rest of the courtroom was so overcome with Joe's obvious pain that women began crying almost in unison. The judge cleared his throat and shifted gears, asking Jack Taggart if the defense had anything it wished to offer.

"Your Honor, my client has submitted letters from colleagues attesting to his kind nature. He will not be making a statement."

Joe could tell Maxwell was tensing up, he was having real trouble with this. Joe looked back to the judge. *Hurry the hell up. Get this done. C'mon... c'mon...c'mon, issue the damn sentence!*

Judge Holmes offered commentary on the letters from Julie and Maxwell's country club buddies, seemingly enjoying the spotlight. After bloviating for another ten minutes, Judge Holmes finally wrapped it up.

"Mr. Maxwell, you did an awful thing to a woman who devoted her life to underprivileged girls, and made that devoted and decent man there, Joe Haise, a widower. I don't know how you will ever live with yourself." Joe could see Maxwell clench his jaw at mention of Joe's name. "Therefore, for all the reasons stated on the record, I hereby order the defendant to spend 10 years in the Illinois State Prison system. Credit for time served. Parole eligibility will be determined by the State of Illinois. We are adjourned."

Joe breathed a sigh of relief he could not conceal from the media, who began rushing to Joe's side the moment the judge said the word, "adjourned." Joe couldn't help but notice Buddy Scott rise from the back of the gallery, slam his file folder shut and storm toward the courtroom doors with his head down. Joe could see Buddy muttering something to himself, but the only phrase he could make out was, "Fucking bullshit." The reporters shouted questions and scribbled furiously, while cameramen jockeyed for position in the throng. One young reporter managed to grab Buddy's lapel. Mistake. Buddy barked that he had, "No goddamn comment," and burst through the courtroom doors. Meanwhile, the Sheriff's Deputies whisked Maxwell away in an instant with Jack Taggart in tow.

Joe smiled, but only barely, and stated to the press that he was pleased with the result and was hoping to resume his life. He felt a tugging on his sleeve; it was Chet, who was motioning to Joe. Joe thanked the media and said he had no further comment. They turned to descend on Bill McDonald, Jack Taggart and Gary Maxwell had already vanished from the courtroom.

Chet whispered in Joe's ear, "Mr. Haise, Mr. Taggart told me that Mr. Maxwell wants to talk to you. Privately."

Chapter 34

Chet and Joe walked to the back of the courtroom. McDonald was holding court in the hallway, so the press left Joe alone. Joe had agreed to accompany Chet without thinking about it, and now was regretting the decision. *No, if Maxwell wants to grovel for my forgiveness, I'll let him.* Chet was rambling on about the benefits of something he called "Restorative Justice," which involved bringing victim and attacker together for a Kumbayah moment. They arrived at the door in the far end of the courtroom and knocked. A moment passed and a large African-American Deputy opened the door and looked them over. "Oh, yeah. Dude said he wants to see you, Mr. Haise."

Joe walked in, leaving Chet standing in the courtroom as the door closed behind him. The bullpen is a large labyrinth of locked cages running the length of the building, where defendants are held and shuttled back and forth to several different courtrooms. Joe passed some cages and was brought to a heavy metal door. The Deputy pulled out a large key and turned the lock. The door opened revealing a small gray room with Gary Maxwell seated at a heavy metal table. Taggart sat on the edge of table and stopped talking as soon as the door opened.

Taggart stood and spoke up. "Mr. Haise. My client tells me he wants to talk to you without me present. I advised against this, but he insisted. He'd like us all to leave, but you can refuse, of course."

Maxwell looked at Joe without blinking; Joe wasn't going to let this lecherous convict intimidate him. Joe nodded and said, "Sure. You can all leave us alone for a few minutes."

The Deputy shot Joe an uneasy look. "Okay, man. But you need me, you hit the panic button on the wall there. He's shackled at the ankles and wrists and secured to the floor, so you should be okay."

"Thank you, Deputy." Joe nodded and the Deputy and Taggart shuffled past Joe and the heavy door closed behind him. Joe locked eyes on Maxwell and took a seat across from him. Joe had never seen him up close before, only a few glances across the courtroom and the dignified pictures the Trib pulled off his company's website. His slightly graying hair was now almost completely white and he lost weight. His face and arms were gray but the skin around his eyes was sallow. Joe had seen that same look from inmates he interviewed in federal prisons over the years, it's the result of being exposed to florescent lighting for 23 hours per day and getting no productive sleep. A few months in jail took a significant toll on Maxwell, Joe wondered how he would handle nearly ten years.

Joe tried to look tough; he was, after all, the widower confronting the bastard killer. Joe waited for some kind of emotional declaration from Gary that he was innocent, coupled with a plea of forgiveness for the adultery. But Maxwell simply folded his hands on the table and leaned forward.

"So, Mr. Haise. Where did you toss the laptop?"

The color drained from Joe's face and his mouth opened slightly. Joe tried to regain his defiant look, but the damage was already done by his initial hesitation. Gary knew. Joe tried to sound confused, but his efforts only confirmed Gary's accusing tone. "Uh, the laptop?"

"You know what I'm talking about, Haise. That laptop disappeared, and I'm guessing you knew what kind of data was on that thing. In fact, I'm betting you were outside my house that night."

Joe considered his options. Was he being recorded? Doubtful, but he needed to act cautiously. Joe looked at Gary, the man who screwed his Tina every day of the week and twice on Sunday, then bragged about it on the internet. Joe narrowed his eyes, leaned forward and whispered to Maxwell, "Gary, where did you toss the cellphones?"

Maxwell sat back, now it was his turn to be knocked off-kilter. He let out a slight laugh and leaned back in. "I jammed them under the seats of each of my daughters' bikes. No time to dump them anywhere else, and the cops never thought to look there when they were turning my house upside down. After I got arrested, Veronica had the movers come the next week and pack everything up. Those bikes are wrapped in bubble

169

wrap sitting in a mover's box in some storage locker waiting for Veronica to complete the move. But when she finds them, whoo boy. Look out." Maxwell was actually relaxed and seemed to be almost at peace being able to talk to the only other person that knew the truth. He gestured around the room with his head, "But this mess here? It's already done, so I don't really care. And hell, I couldn't prove you did anything, or that you even *knew* anything. I dropped your name to my lawyer as a possible suspect, but no one really turned up anything, so I let it pass until I knew what my options were. Then I get handed this here plea deal, and hell, ten years and a wakeup with a minimal civil settlement with your lawyer Baker was better than risking everything by giving the DA motive for murder if I blabbed about my little 'business arrangement' with your wife. So I kept my mouth shut. "

Joe was trying to stay composed, but Maxwell was way ahead of him and Joe was playing catch-up. "I see. So you and Tina were, well-acquainted?"

Joe regretted the question immediately, he could tell Maxwell was relishing the opportunity to twist the knife on the man who just put him in prison for 10 years. "Oh, yeah. She was a sweet piece, let me tell you. A real spinner. I was a good customer for her for a couple of years. And right under your nose the whole time, too. God, you were clueless. And you know, I am guessing she was willing to do shit with me that you never got to. In fact, I know that's true. And any time I told her how special she was, how she could be a player in the circles I ran in, how she could ditch her Leave It To Beaver life and open up an international fashion house or a national ballet production or some such bullshit, she'd get soaking wet, throw her legs in the air and we would totally get off together."

Joe balled up his fist and began huffing. "You cocksucker. I hope you rot."

Maxwell became more serene as Joe became more enraged. Now Maxwell was acting like a professor lecturing a student, tenting his fingers and looking thoughtfully at the ceiling. "Well, I really won't rot, Joe. I can do this time pretty quick, and I'll be back on my feet. But what about you, Joe? You are a narcissist, did you know that? I can always spot one. I'm betting you never thought about anything but yourself. Your wife, on the

170

other hand, only wanted someone to feed her aspirations. That's why a girl like Alessandra, I mean, *Tina*, was such easy pickings for us. Do you know that the money meant nothing to her? Hell, she even forgot to ask me for payment one time. What kind of a pro does that? Forgets to ask for the money? Nope, I think she *liked* the sex, but she *loved* the attention. Got off on it. You, my friend, offered her a prison in Libertyville with a life sentence. And me, I let her drone on about Milan, Paris, Barcelona, blah, blah, blah. And after the sex, she would lie in my arms and nuzzle my neck as she talked. She would kiss me deeply and…"

Joe bolted out of his chair and frantically banged on the door. "Deputy?! Deputy!" Joe was desperate to escape.

Gary was laughing hysterically when the Deputy finally opened the door. Joe nearly knocked him over as he ran past a confused Jack Taggart. Gary's demented laughter reverberated off the walls and chased after Joe down the corridor. Joe slammed into the iron door leading to the court-room and tried in vain to pry the handle open. The Deputy ran after Joe, fumbling for his keys before finally unlocking the door and pulling it open. Joe ran through the courtroom, rushed past Chet and bolted for the eleva-tor, frantically punching the button for the parking garage. By the time he made it to his car, he was throwing up next to the trunk. Joe cleaned him-self up, climbed in and started the engine. He began sobbing as he drove away with Maxwell's laughter echoing in his ears.

Chapter 35

Joe spent the rest of the day in bed. He smelled the sheets repeatedly hoping to catch Tina's scent, but he washed them a dozen times since the murder and the bed smelled like Tide, nothing else. His phone buzzed a few times from numbers he didn't recognize, probably reporters. He tossed it aside and remained in bed. Joe called Dr. Phillips for a refill of his valium, which was quickly called in to the Walgreens down the street. Joe drove there in a t-shirt and sweatpants, picked up the prescription and popped two pills in the parking lot before even starting the car.

Joe spent the next three days in bed, putting away four or five pills each day and a bottle of red wine each night. Dave Dunham told Joe to take all the time he needed, and Joe took him up on the offer. Joe dreamt of Tina at night, she was always alone in a large empty room and she was coughing. Joe was searching for a glass of water for her but couldn't find one. He kept telling her that he was sorry but she just kept coughing. He woke up sweating and feeling constricted.

He thought about Tina, their wedding, the wake. In the end, no one really cared. She was not a dynamic personality whose loss would ripple across friends and family for years. Tina was like any of the faceless summer interns Joe worked with at the US Attorney's Office: she was there for a while, she made a few acquaintances then she simply went away and was forgotten by everyone five minutes after she walked out the door. Whatever it was that made her tick died with her. Joe wasn't sure what he was supposed to do about that.

By Thursday, Joe started to recover a bit. He thought about Maxwell and what he said. Whenever Joe started to engage in some kind of introspection, his hate for Maxwell overtook his thoughts. *Who the hell is he to judge? He is a convicted murderer. And an adulterer. Fuck him, I hope the Aryans or the Latin Kings sell his tight ass for cigarettes in the prison canteen.* Joe's anger began to rise and he managed to get out of bed and take his first shower since Monday.

Joe went to his basement and collected all the boxes marked "Tina." He marched to his driveway and threw them in the garbage bin. He threw out the empty bottles of red wine and tossed the bottle of valium in the desk drawer. He went into Tina's old office and started to exercise again.

Joe woke up early the next morning and made it in to work for the first time all week. It was Friday, so there was a lighter mood in the office and he was greeted with a lot of supportive smiles as he walked in, even getting two long hugs from Stacey Wozniak and her ample cleavage. Joe was getting his swagger back. Dave Dunham welcomed back his "pit bull," Joe liked the sound of that. Joe waited for Jackie Dekker to stop by his office, but after an hour with no sign of her he grew annoyed. Joe walked to her office, but the lights were off. He walked back to the lobby and stopped at Stacey's desk.

"Stace? Where is Jackie Dekker?"

"Umm, she took a personal day. She had a dental appointment this morning and then she had to see her niece's school play. She'll be back Monday I guess."

"Oh, okay. Thanks." Joe returned to his office and closed the door. He turned to his computer and began catching up on emails. A few minutes passed and Joe grew bored. He made a few strategic clicks and opened the Provocateur Courtesans website. He called up Alessandra's profile, it was still available. Because no one knew who she was, there was no need to delete it. He stared at the half-naked pictures and reread the list of what she was willing to do for money. He reread "Gary M.'s" customer review and smiled. *Serves both of 'em right.* Joe spent the rest of the day on the computer checking and rechecking the Courtesan's website, surfing the other women's profiles and seeing if he missed anything in between rounds of Minesweeper. He began wondering about the other women listed. *Natasha is a physician in central Illinois who did some modeling in medical school.* Tina's mom lives in Peoria, which is in Central Illinois. Perhaps he should pay Midge a visit, maybe think of something to do with his spare time while he's down

173

there. Joe hadn't noticed the office growing dark. He checked his watch, it was 7:30 p.m. Joe walked out to the hallway and the office was vacant. He cleared his browser history and powered down the computer, turned out the lights, grabbed his coat and sauntered to the elevator.

Joe was a few miles north of the office when he made a detour and headed back downtown. He went to the department store and greeted the same cute brunette clerk that talked him into buying his cologne the month before. She didn't remember him, but he flirted with her anyway as she rang up his purchase. Joe scooped up the bag, jumped in his car and peeled out of the lot.

Several hours later Joe realized his life seemed to be making sense again. Perhaps even more sense than before, as if he had been awakened from a lifelong slumber and now was ready to climb into this new persona and take it out for a spin. He was back in control, all his little office chickens were in the coop where he could keep an eye on them. He smiled at the gift bag in his lap and removed its contents: a bottle of Coco by Chanel body lotion. *She will like this*, Joe thought. He pulled out his phone and began texting.

Hey Jackie! Just finished some stuff tonight on our fraud case, we'll get 'em!

Joe pressed "send" and stared at the screen. He waited as the minutes ticked by; after an eternity, his phone lit up and a ding announced the arrival of a text.

You bet, Joe! See you Monday! Nite nite!

Joe leaned out of his driver's side window and stared at the modest second story apartment across the street. A figure moved across the shade and turned off the light, Joe settled back in his seat. *Night, Jackie.*

Chicago Two-Step
Point Of View Trilogy Vol. II: Jackie Dekker

Watch for the second installment of the Point Of View Trilogy by J. Thomas Ganzer: Chicago Two Step - Jackie Dekker, scheduled for release in 2014!

Chapter 1

Jackie Dekker was having the worst day in recorded history. Well, perhaps top three. Marie Antoinette had her head lopped off by a bunch of filthy French peasants and Anne Boleyn suffered a similar fate for her failure to give her corpulent husband King Henry VIII a male heir. Jackie considered her company and accepted third place on that list. First, her alarm clock refused to go off and she woke up 30 minutes late. She spilled coffee on her lucky trial suit and had to switch to a wrinkled backup from the laundry pile that smelled funky. Her hair developed a cowlick overnight, which she is pretty sure is not possible as far as the physics of the human scalp goes. She caught her stocking on the car door and developed a run that a drop of clear nail polish could never save. She then spent the entire drive to the Federal Courthouse in Chicago trying to smooth out her hair and managed to spill coffee on her skirt. Again. She got off the elevator, ran into her office and dropped everything on her desk, grabbed her banker's box and a legal pad and sprinted to the elevator.

In the only piece of luck for the morning, she breathlessly arrived at court on time. The defense attorney was shaking hands with his clients, suggesting he just arrived as well. The clerk and court reporter were not there yet, so Jackie had a few minutes to get settled. She unpacked her box and saw the defense attorney walking toward her. She tried to slow her breathing and stuck her hand out energetically, "Hello Jerome!"

"Ms. Dekker, it's good to see you again." He is much calmer than Jackie; presumably at some point between your fourth year out of law school, like Jackie, and your 20th year, like Jerome Luckett, you stop getting excited about jury trials. Jackie looked across at Luckett's clients, they squinted and frowned disapprovingly in unison. Having people that don't know anything about you hate every single inch of your slimy guts was something she would have to get used to as a federal prosecutor. The older couple, a tall slender man and a short, portly woman, sat down in their chairs and stared straight ahead. Jackie sat down, opened the case file for the thousandth time, and read an FBI report that she could probably recite from memory by now.

Murray Lefkowicz, a gangly, odd-looking man in his 60s, loved to spend his days in the public libraries of Chicago's northwest suburbs. He drew the attention of the librarians who immediately assumed he was a pedophile. But the intensity at which he stared at financial websites all day allayed their concerns. Hour after hour, day after day, Murray stared at the computer. Always the same tattered clothes, always the same worn out shoes. One day, Murray walked in, nodded to the staff that had come to expect him at precisely 9:30 a.m., sat down at the computer and removed a letter from his pocket. The crisp paper and colorful letterhead from the large financial services firm congratulated Murray on passing the Series 7 test, which allowed Murray to begin work as a licensed stockbroker. The advisor sponsored Murray's application for the exam through a charitable program run by the City of Chicago called "Fourth Chance," which Jackie concluded is the least inspirational name for a charitable group, ever. The Mayor supported the program with photo ops and tax breaks for the sponsors. The program is designed to get older military veterans with financial need started in brand new careers.

The letter went on to say that by passing the test, Murray is no longer eligible for the financial company's work-study program and, unfortunately, they don't have a job for him and he needs to clear out his cubby by Friday. Murray folded the letter and tucked it into his pocket. Murray knew weeks ago that this would happen and he had been preparing for this moment ever since. He walked over to a bookshelf, withdrew a large volume and returned to his desk. He moved the mouse and clicked the State of

176

Illinois website. While the page loaded, he flipped open the World Atlas he took from the shelf and opened to the section on Great Britain. Murray would later confess that he believed people who lived in London and worked in the financial district were obviously good with money and he wanted to honor them. After thumbing through the pages on London suburbs, Murray's eyes lit up and he pivoted to the keyboard. Murray found a suburb called Kingston Upon Thames and later told the FBI that "... it sounds like a place where rich people go..." Murray fished around his pocket, nervously withdrew his tattered wallet and pulled out his Farmers Bank of Streator Visa, with its mighty $1,500 limit, and entered the payment information on the Illinois Secretary of State website. With a click of the mouse, Murray officially registered Kingston Upon Thames Investments, LLC.

Murray then scanned a few more website forums and, after spending time on the Better Business Bureau website, paid the appropriate membership fee for "accreditation." He added a few anonymous comments attesting to the brilliant investment advisors of Kingston Upon Thames Investments. Murray was relatively certain that his new venture would earn an "A" rating from the BBB in short order. Next, Murray realized he needed an accountant to balance his books but he was quickly running out of available credit. Murray would have to set up an accounting firm that would exist in cyberspace only. Looking back at the Atlas, Murray concluded that "...rich people golf and golf started in Scotland." Murray found two spectacular golf courses outside of Edinburgh, Musselburgh Golf Club and Prestonfield Golf Course, and with that, Musselburgh & Prestonfield Accounting, LLP, was formed (sort of). A few more hours at a website and domain starter and the websites for each were up and running. In spite of Murray's spelling mistakes, the websites looked passable.

Murray decided he needed a law firm to handle the complex global financial empire he was building in the young adult section of the Gail Borden Public Library. But what country has the best lawyers in Europe? When Murray was briefly in prison (the result of a disagreement with the Revenuers over the propriety of certain tax deductions), he met a lawyer from Germany named Hans. Hans was a nice guy who had a thing for "jerkin' the gherkin" in the parking lot of a junior high in Mundelein. Murray flipped to the section showing Berlin and its suburbs. The Atlas described several rather cosmopolitan-sounding boroughs northeast of Berlin, and heretofore henceforth Murray was now represented *per se* by the law firm of Marzahn & Hellersdorf, SC. After using his superior skills to create a letterhead for his new army of barristers (or whatever the Germans called them), Murray was off to Kinko's. Two hours later and with his credit card nearly maxed out, Murray walked out with his investment company's prospectus, business cards, bid proposal on colorful letterhead, a detailed report from his accountant testifying to the healthy cash reserves and real estate holdings of the investment firm, and a report from his alleged law firm afore described that detailed his network of ownership interests. The bid letter was proudly signed by Series 7 licensee Murry R. Lefkowicz.

About the Author

J. Thomas Ganzer is an attorney practicing in Milwaukee, Wisconsin. He handled civil and criminal matters in private practice and at the Wisconsin Department of Justice. He currently practices civil litigation for the Milwaukee Metropolitan Sewerage District. This is his first novel, and this work of fiction should be treated gently.

Contact Information
Joseph T. Ganzer
7935 Eagle Street
Wauwatosa, WI 53213
608-628-8803
jtganzer@gmail.com

www.ingramcontent.com/pod-product-compliance
Lightning Source LLC
Chambersburg PA
CBHW022119170626
46808CB00002B/780